I DREAM OF CHRISTMAS

A HEARTSPRINGS VALLEY WINTER TALE (BOOK 4)

ANNE CHASE

THOMAS PUBLISHING

ISBN-13: 978-1-945320-09-5

For Pat and Mary Kay

*M*elody Connelly emerged from the cab and gasped as bone-chilling winter air invaded her lungs. She loved New York — its energy and vitality and craziness were fuel for her restless soul — but winter was *not* its best look. Pulling her coat tight around her neck, she dashed into the lobby of the Grand Astoria Hotel, a gust of wind roaring in with her, eager to make its presence felt.

As she strode inside, she shook her tumble of red hair, shaking off the cold as she did so. Even at this early hour, the lobby was buzzing with guests checking in and checking out, friends greeting friends, and businesspeople meeting their contacts.

Everywhere she looked, Christmas decorations — poinsettias and wreaths and ornaments galore —

announced that her favorite holiday of the year was just around the corner.

With confident steps, she slipped through the bustle, pausing briefly as she passed a wall mirror to straighten her back and arrange her expression into her "star" face: friendly without being too friendly, welcoming without being too welcoming. A face that, when photographed, would appear natural and appealing.

She had a lot to be thankful for when it came to her appearance — high cheekbones, a good nose, unblemished skin, vivacious green eyes, a wide, expressive mouth, and of course the beautiful red hair. But no one was immune to a bad photo, a lesson she'd learned through hard-won experience.

Satisfied that her persona of friendly, relatable Broadway star was firmly in place, she strode into Le Perq, the hottest breakfast spot in New York. The manager saw her immediately and rushed up.

"Mademoiselle Connelly, good morning!"

"Good morning, Henri," she said with a warm smile. "How are you this morning?"

"Fine, mademoiselle, just fine, thank you." He grabbed a menu and gestured toward the dining room. "Your breakfast companion arrived a few moments ago."

She followed him in, aware of her fellow diners pretending not to notice. As a noted Broadway performer, she was famous, of course, but she was *their* famous — one of their own. Someone whose presence they understood they should act nonchalant about.

The room was as sleek and modern as ever, but in honor of the season it now sported a few touches of Christmas. Silver wreaths hung on the walls. In a corner stood a silver Christmas tree with softly glowing white lights.

Very pretty, Melody thought instantly, *but not nearly warm enough.*

Ahead of them, at one of the room's best tables, she spied her breakfast companion sipping his morning tea.

A rush of affection flowed through her. Nigel Farraday was such a dear — a wiz with public relations and a sweetheart to boot. A rumpled man with thinning hair and a perpetually frazzled expression, he was dressed today in his usual tweed suit and red bow tie.

He rose from the table and greeted her with an air kiss on each cheek. "My dear," he said, "radiant as always."

"Nigel, you're looking so trim!"

He grimaced. "It's this new diet of Pamela's," he said, referring to his wife, whom Melody adored. He stared at his waist as if shocked by what he wasn't seeing.

"Yes, I know," Melody replied. "She called this

morning. Asked me to report if you order anything unhealthy."

Nigel scowled. "One bad number from the doctor and suddenly everything good is off-limits. What is the point of living if one can't have what one desires?"

"Pamela and your doctor just want what's best."

They settled into their seats and, after Melody ordered coffee, they quickly perused the menu.

Nigel threw her a baleful look. "The pancakes here are sensational."

"So is the oatmeal." She gave him a smile. "Trust, darling. Utterly delish."

"Look at this one," Nigel whispered, pointing to a menu item, his tone pleading. "Eggs Benedict with pork loin...."

"Nigel," she said patiently.

"Oh, all right," he growled. "I will accede, temporarily, to the combined tyrannies of marriage and modern medicine."

Melody smiled and gestured to the waiter. "Two of your house oatmeals, please."

With that settled, Nigel scanned the room with a professional eye.

"Who are you looking for?" Melody asked.

"No one in particular," he replied. Which wasn't really true. He'd selected this location because it was *the* current Manhattan breakfast hot spot — the perfect place to make new connections and pursue business deals.

"You look worried," Melody said, watching him run his hand through his sparse hair.

"Only about your career, my dear. This plan of yours to take a break — it worries me."

"I'm sure everything will work out fine."

"Mmm," he said, pursing his lips, clearly disagreeing. Nigel was a genius at making things happen — he had a gift for divining opportunities out of thin air — but he needed a client who was willing to play along.

And right now, the last thing Melody wanted to do was *play along*. For the past eight months, her life had been a nonstop, full-on, high-energy rush of rehearsals and performances and promotional events — rewarding and meaningful, to be sure, but also exhausting.

Just two nights earlier, she'd given her final performance as the originating star of Broadway's newest musical smash, *Manhattan on the Rocks*. She'd taken her bows, basked in the accolades, and stepped gratefully off the stage.

And now she was focused on a single goal:

Escaping north, to the little town that had captured her heart, where she would soon be hosting the ultimate holiday family gathering.

Because *this* was the year she'd finally do Christmas right.

As if reading her mind, Nigel said, "It's this town you've taken under your wing, isn't it? This … Heartsprings Valley." He said it like it was a pest, a nuisance he couldn't get rid of.

"You think I'm crazy to have bought a house up there."

"Yes, completely mad. I believe the word is 'bonkers.'"

"Oh, you. It's wonderful up there."

"I will grant, as hamlets go, the place is rather charming," Nigel allowed. "A jewel of small-town coziness, if you go for that sort of thing." He gave a little shudder. "Though I can't see how anyone would."

Melody smiled. Truth be told, she suspected Nigel held a grudge. Two years earlier, his assistant Clara had announced her intention to quit her New York job and return to her hometown of Heartsprings Valley. Ever since, Nigel had been searching in vain for an assistant with Clara's mix of brains, organizational chops, and inexhaustible patience — someone who could keep up with (and *put* up with) his unique blend of marketing genius and personal inattentiveness.

"I've met some amazing people up there, thanks to Clara," Melody said. "People who have become dear friends."

"And I'm happy for you, dear, of course I am. But people in Heartsprings Valley do not produce movies or TV series. People in Heartsprings Valley do not sign artists to recording contracts. People in Heartsprings Valley milk cows and bake cookies and chop wood and grow corn and...."

Melody burst out laughing. "Oh, Nigel. You're being silly. You have to come up and spend some time. You and Pamela and the kids. The house is almost ready. There's plenty of room."

"Me, dear? You'll take me *hiking* or some such."

"I'll introduce you to some cows. The ones you're apparently afraid of."

A gleam came to his eye. "It all sounds very organic. Down-to-earth. Back to nature. Finding one's roots. Returning to a simpler way of life."

"You've just had a brainstorm, haven't you?"

He leaned forward. "I see you with a cow. You'll have to befriend a cow. A cow named Daisy. I see the two of you in a beautiful green field, the sun shining, the air clear, the sky blue. Daisy's chewing cud — is that what cows do? — while you look at the camera and extol the virtues of nature or fresh food or some such."

"Nigel...."

"I see a healthy glow in your cheeks. You're relaxed. The simple life, personified. Viewers will eat it up."

"You're talking — what? A sponsorship? TV commercials?"

He waved her question away. "Scads of companies would die to have you as their spokesperson. The most beautiful voice on Broadway, singing their praises? I'll round up some media — the usual suspects — to trumpet your new life in your little town. You'll be cresting a wave."

"What wave?"

"The health wave. The simplicity wave. The back-to-what's-real wave. I know waves, my dear. You leave that to me."

Their oatmeal arrived and they dug in. Nigel chewed slowly, a look of concentration on his face. "This is rather good, actually," he conceded.

"Glad to hear."

Nigel glanced over her shoulder and went still. His shrewd eyes, now filled with concern, darted back to her. "I hate to ask," he said quietly, "but is anything going on again with you and Derek?"

Melody frowned. "No, of course not. Why do you ask?"

"Because he's here," Nigel murmured. "And headed our way."

CHAPTER 2

*M*elody froze. A jolt of anxiety shot through her. She forced herself to *not* turn around and do what she knew, without a doubt, every other person in the restaurant was doing at that very moment:

Gawking at the huge movie star in their midst.

Derek Davies was, by any measure, one of the most famous human beings on the planet. His action flicks, packed with thrills and humor, wowed audiences and critics alike. Almost effortlessly, year after year, his blazing good looks, self-deprecating charm, and fondness for impressive stunts ruled the summer box office.

Two years earlier, for a brief moment, he and Melody had been an item. Okay, more than an item. The breakup had hurt. She'd allowed herself to get caught up in the excitement, the rush, the whirlwind of early romance. She'd allowed herself to be vulnerable. She'd allowed herself to *feel*.

Around her, the room hushed. Nobody, it seemed, wanted to miss what happened next. Without looking up, she sensed that Derek had reached her table.

Nigel broke the ice. "Derek, long time no see."

Melody looked up. Her former beau was gazing right at her, handsome as ever, his blue eyes flashing energy and interest.

Derek nodded briefly at Nigel — "Nigel, good to see you" — then returned his attention to her.

"Hello, Melody."

Her chest tightened. She'd forgotten how charismatic he was, especially up close.

Breathe, she told herself. *Breathe.*

"Hello, Derek," she replied, relieved to hear herself sounding calm and composed.

"You look great."

"Thank you." He looked great as well, with his short-cropped brown hair and chiseled jaw, his skin tanned from wherever he'd been recently. He was dressed for winter in New York — black boots and dark jeans, with a grey wool sweater hugging his broad shoulders.

He gave her a small smile. "Congratulations on your new show."

"Thank you." He'd sent flowers for her closing

performance — she'd wondered why. "And thank you for the flowers. They were lovely."

"I caught your final show."

"I didn't know that," she said, surprised.

"I didn't say anything because I figured...." He let the words remain unspoken. He seemed abashed. "I was hoping we could ... talk. Have coffee."

Melody's eyebrows rose. "Talk? About what?"

Derek glanced around the room. "Past mistakes. *My* past mistakes."

A rebellious flare of emotion — what kind of emotion, she wasn't sure — rushed through her. Ruthlessly, she pushed it down.

"I don't know," she said. "I'm about to head out of town...."

"To your new second home." When he saw her surprise, he added, "I've been following what's going on with you."

She stared at him, flummoxed. "You've been following what's going on with me?"

He nodded, very simply. One of Derek's strengths as an actor — and he was a good actor — was his ability to convey emotion without moving a muscle on his face, using only his eyes to radiate whatever feeling was required, be it joy or sorrow or anger or confusion or shock or flirtatious interest. Right now, his eyes were conveying *regret*.

"I know I screwed up," he said. "I'd like to make amends."

Melody swallowed. Of all the things she might have imagined happening at breakfast this morning, a surprise run-in with her ex was not among them. And for Derek to be so direct, so open, so up-front about the mistake he'd made….

"I don't know what to say," she finally said.

"Please say you'll have coffee with me," he said, ramping up the charm.

"I'll think about it."

"How about this afternoon?"

"Sorry, I can't. I'm picking up my mom at the airport after lunch, and then we're heading up north for Christmas."

"To that new town of yours?"

"Yes, Heartsprings Valley."

He hesitated, unsure how to proceed. It wasn't often that people didn't give him exactly what he wanted.

"Listen, Derek," she said. "I appreciate what you said, and I'll be happy to have coffee with you."

"Just not today," he said, his gaze intensifying.

"That's right."

"Okay. Got it." He clapped his hands together, somewhat awkwardly, then gestured to his table. "I should probably get back to…."

"It was good seeing you, Derek."

"See you soon?"

Melody gave him a small smile. "See you soon."

CHAPTER 3

*W*ould she? See him soon?
Did she even want to?

Melody growled softly to herself. Breakfast was over and she was back in her apartment, staring at the suitcase lying open on her bed, trying to figure out what she'd forgotten to pack. Something was missing — but what? It was suddenly hard to concentrate. The day was moving forward relentlessly, the pale light of midday filtering through the windows. Her mom's flight would land soon. She needed to get to the airport. But her suitcase was demanding her attention. Which was tough to give when her mind kept returning to her morning surprise.

Nigel, bless his heart, hadn't pressed or pried, though he must have been tempted. A rekindled romance with Hollywood royalty represented a public-relations bonanza. The media attention would be phenomenal, the business opportunities staggering.

Instead, after Derek left them, Nigel had quietly said, "He made a huge mistake two years ago. He doesn't deserve you." Then, tactfully and adroitly, he'd changed the subject to business and, for the rest of their breakfast, kept Melody focused on an avalanche of media and promotional ideas. When they parted, he extracted a promise from her to stay open to new opportunities even as she enjoyed her winter break in Heartsprings Valley. "When I call, young lady," he said as he gave her a hug, "I expect you to pick up the phone. I do not want to hear you're too busy baking scones or ice skating or decorating your Christmas tree or some such."

"Oh, Nigel," she'd said with a laugh. "Don't be a grouch. I hope you and Pamela and the kids have a wonderful Christmas."

"Same to you, my dear. I hope your Christmas is everything you dream of."

The thought came then: *her scarves!* She rushed to her closet and picked out three of her favorites: one a lovely Christmas red, one a lovely winter green, and the third a floral pattern of blue and cream that went with multiple outfits and contrasted nicely with her hair.

She'd already double-checked to confirm she had the rest of her winter gear: long coat, short coat, boots, mittens, gloves, cap, and now scarves. She had outfits for every occasion already loaded in her SUV downstairs, along with a shopping bag bursting with Christmas gifts for her new friends up north. She had her phone and her laptop and her reading tablet and —

Books! She reached across her bed and grabbed her latest read, a Nero Wolfe mystery she'd snagged in a bookstore. Before fame and success had found her, back when she was just a struggling actor-singer-waiter, she'd haunted the city's used bookstores, seeking escape and entertainment at bargain-basement prices. She missed doing that — missed the pleasure of stumbling across a tattered copy of a favorite book or discovering a book she knew nothing about, and deciding, as she held it in her hands, that she was going to give it a try....

She made one last walk-through to ensure everything was right and ready. Her apartment wasn't large — two bedrooms, a bathroom, a galley kitchen, and an open dining-living area with south-facing windows that brought in tons of natural light — but it was all hers and she treasured it. An actor pal had jumped at the chance to play house-sitter while she was away; her collection of potted plants would be in good hands.

With a satisfied sigh, she closed her suitcase, maneuvered it to the floor, and grabbed hold of the handle. She was almost at the door when she felt her phone vibrate. She reached into her jacket pocket and saw a single word:

Mom.

She picked up. "Hi, Mom," she said. "What's up? Everything okay?"

"Are you in your apartment?" her mom said. The call signal was faint, her voice scratchy.

"Heading to the airport now to pick you up."

"Benny and I are still in Atlanta," her mom said. "Our flight got canceled."

"Oh, no!"

"We rebooked on a flight first thing tomorrow," her mom continued. "Benny got us a room for the night here, near the airport."

Melody sighed and let go of her suitcase. "I guess that means we'll drive up tomorrow instead of today."

"No, no, no," her mom said right away. "We know how much you want to get up there. You go on up. Benny reserved an SUV. We'll drive up tomorrow."

"No need for that, Mom."

"We'll be fine. We like long drives. I hear it's beautiful up there."

Melody considered pushing back but heard the finality in her mother's voice. From a lifetime of experience, she knew the window for arguing had passed. "If you say so, Mom," she said reluctantly. "Are you sure?"

"Absolutely. You get yourself up there and make sure everything's ready for us. I know you're itching to get up there."

Melody smiled. How true that was. For the past eight months, in every spare moment, she'd done her best to keep track of the renovations at her new house, learning more than she ever knew was possible about load-bearing walls and I-beams and wet insulation and scads of other construction terms and techniques.

"Well," Melody said. "I guess that makes sense. Have you checked the weather report?"

"The forecast is fine. Don't you worry. We'll see you tomorrow."

"Call when you land in New York, and drive safely."

"Will do."

"Give my best to Benny. Love you."

"Love you, too, dear. See you tomorrow."

And then she was gone. Melody stared at her phone for a moment, as if willing it back to life, then slipped it into her coat pocket and grabbed her suitcase.

Her mom was right. A tingle of excitement coursed through her.

With a bounce in her step, she headed out the door.

Heartsprings Valley, here I come!

CHAPTER 4

*D*ay was slipping to dusk as Melody crested the ridge overlooking Heartsprings Valley. The drive from New York had been smooth and uneventful — wonderfully so. She missed being behind the wheel — the roar of the engine when she hit the gas, the jolts and bumps of the road, the scenery flashing by. She drove so rarely now. Life in the theater meant sacrifice, including everyday things she'd always taken for granted. Her poor SUV spent most of its time neglected and alone, stuck in the darkness of her building's garage.

She felt a pang of guilt and immediately chastised herself. Such a silly thought to have. A car was a piece of machinery. It didn't feel or think. It didn't have the ability to be *lonely*. Nevertheless, she gave the dashboard a pat and said, "You're going to like being back up here — so much to see and do." The car responded with a happy rumble.

She'd been looking forward to this trip for months. Even as *Manhattan on the Rocks* consumed nearly every waking moment, her planned escape from New York had been ever-present, a mental dream list with items eager to be checked off:

Get through the final performance of her latest show: *Check*.

Plan the perfect Christmas with her mother: *Check*.

Finish her new house: *Oh, so close*.

Figure out the next chapter in her life: *Gulp!*

The twists and turns of the ridge road began smoothing out as she got closer to the main road that ran through the valley. An early winter snow lay like dust on the ground, glowing faintly in the darkness. She fiddled with the dial until she landed on the local radio station, sighing happily as "It's Beginning to Look a Lot Like Christmas" washed over her. She sang along, spirits soaring, as she passed farmhouses and barns decorated for the season.

Gladness filled her heart: *She was here!* She'd missed this place so much. Holiday lights appeared in greater profusion as she got closer to town, brightening the dark night with bursts of color. Many of the displays were quite exuberant. She passed a farmhouse with a life-size Santa, his sleigh and reindeer touching down next to the chimney. On a nearby barn, red and green and white lights blanketed every inch of the roof. Snowmen were everywhere, of course — Heartsprings Valley loved its snowpeople and snow animals. She grinned at a cheerful fellow in a field near the side of the road, wearing a top hat, corncob pipe, and button nose, holding up a big sign that said, "Smile! It's Christmas!"

She'd been charmed by this little town during her first visit up here, two Christmases ago. Now, without question, it held a piece of her heart.

One of the big reasons was up ahead, just minutes away. As she drove through the quiet residential neighborhood on the outskirts of town, her excitement increased. She made a right turn and saw her destination: a grand Queen Anne-style residence on a corner lot, painted pale blue with crisp white trim, boasting a wide wraparound porch, a Dutch gable roof, and a circular tower topped with a rooster weathervane. Through a window, she caught a glimpse of a colorful Christmas tree.

The sign out front said simply, "Heartsprings Valley Inn." But to her, this beautiful place meant so much more. Two years earlier, still in shock from her breakup with Derek, the Inn had become an unlikely refuge — a safe harbor where she was able to nurse her wounds, a place where she'd been welcomed with open arms.

She spied a parking spot out front and eased in. "We're here," she said to the car. With a grateful sigh, she turned off the engine and allowed the silence to wash over her, enjoying the hush and sense of anticipation.

In the coming days, she would be busy — joyfully busy, if her plans came to fruition. This moment of quiet might be the last she'd experience until the holidays were over. But her excitement couldn't be contained. Without bothering to grab her coat, she opened the door, inhaling sharply as cold winter air filled her lungs, and dashed up the stone path to the Inn's porch. A big Christmas wreath on the heavy oak front door sported a hand-written sign: "Come on in!" With a push, she made her way inside. Immediately, the warmth and aroma of chocolate chip cookies greeted her.

"Yoo-hoo!" she said as she closed the door behind her, her stage voice projecting effortlessly. "Barbara? Stu? I've arrived!"

A clanging of pots came from the kitchen. A familiar and beloved head popped into the hallway.

"Melody!" Barbara said. "You made it!" The inn owner bustled up, arms outstretched, and pulled Melody in for a big hug. She was a tall woman — about Melody's height — with lively brown eyes, short brown hair flecked with gray, and a mouth that grinned at a second's notice. As usual, she was dressed in jeans, holiday sweater, and apron. Although Barbara loved everything about running a bed-and-breakfast, her preferred domain was the kitchen.

"So glad to see you!" Melody said, returning the hug.

"And you! Any troubles on the way up?"

"The drive was lovely."

"Good." Barbara looked behind Melody. "Your bags?"

"In the car. I'll get them later."

"Stu's out getting supplies. He can help when he gets back."

Barbara led Melody by the arm into the kitchen. "We have so much to catch up on."

"I'm so happy to be back up here."

"You must be excited about your big Christmas plans."

"Oh, I am. And maybe a tad nervous."

"I'm sure everything will work out just fine."

The kitchen was just as Melody remembered: spacious and welcoming and going full-tilt. On the stove, a pot full of potatoes was boiling away. On the countertop, a tray of freshly baked chocolate-chip cookies lay resting. The lovely scent of honey-glazed ham wafted from one of Barbara's two ovens.

Barbara inspected the boiling potatoes. "Dinner tonight is ham, mashed potatoes, and spinach, plus all the usual fixings."

"What can I do to help?"

"I knew you'd ask. Never shy about pitching in

— I noticed that about you from the start. Why don't you do the spinach?"

"In the fridge?"

"Yep. I chopped fresh garlic earlier — there on the counter."

Melody rinsed her hands in the sink. "How are you? How's the Inn? How's Stu?"

"Oh, we're all fine. Keeping busy like always."

"How's business?"

"Good. We were almost fully booked all fall."

"Glad to hear. I can't believe I haven't seen you since the spring."

"Time flies." Barbara shook her head ruefully. "Seems to move faster every day."

Melody turned off the faucet and grabbed a towel to dry off. She'd grown so fond of Barbara over the past two years. From the moment they met, they'd had a rapport, an instant comfort, that she cherished.

Barbara turned off the burner beneath the pot of potatoes. "We're putting your mom in the room next to yours."

"That's great."

"She and her husband will be up tomorrow?"

"Late afternoon or early evening."

"And her husband's name is Benny?" Barbara asked. She took hold of the pot and carefully poured the hot water into the sink.

"That's right. Benny Brankowski."

"How long have they been married?"

"Three years." Melody smiled. "And I'm relieved to report that I like him."

Barbara glanced over. "You sound surprised."

"I guess I am," Melody confessed. "Let's just say Mom's always had a knack for picking the wrong guys."

"The wrong guys?"

Melody sighed. Talking about her mom was never easy. Though, to be fair, in the past couple of years, talking about her had become … less complex. "I think what I mean is, the guys were wrong for her. It's not that they were criminals or anything like that. They just weren't the right fit."

"Give me an example," Barbara said as she started mashing the potatoes.

"Okay," she said as she grabbed a bag of spinach from the fridge. "Before Benny, Mom was dating Jim, who was a big sailing fanatic. For him, it was all about his sailboat. Every chance he got, he was out in the Gulf."

"That could be fun."

"Mom enjoyed it, especially at first. She'd never spent much time on the water. They'd go out sailing for an afternoon and have a great time. They even took a two-week sailing trip down to Key West, stopping in towns along the way, and she loved it."

"So why was he not the right fit for her?"

Melody grabbed a skillet and set it on a burner.

"What he really wanted was for her to join him on an around-the-world sailing trip."

"Oh, my." Barbara tossed a dash of butter into the potatoes and returned to mashing.

"Mom insisted she wanted to go. I tried to persuade her to not jump in so quickly — they'd only been dating a few months — but she wouldn't hear it."

"What happened?"

"She went anyway."

"And?"

"By the time they docked in Jamaica, she'd seen the light."

"Oh, my."

Melody drizzled olive oil in the skillet, then added garlic. "She flew home from Kingston alone, feeling guilty and disappointed in herself."

"Disappointed because...?"

"She'd made yet another mistake, and she knew it. It's part of her pattern. She meets a guy, she gets all excited, she goes all in, and when it doesn't work out, she beats herself up."

"We all have our patterns, don't we?" Barbara murmured.

"Truer words, darling," Melody said as she opened the bag of spinach and watched the leaves tumble out. "Truer words."

Steam rose from the skillet, bringing with it a lovely garlic aroma.

"But this Benny fellow," Barbara said. "I take it he's not a mistake?"

"That's right," Melody said, her mood brightening. "He's actually *not* a mistake."

"She finally picked right. Where'd they meet?"

"In Tallahassee, where Mom lives. At a retirement party for a mutual friend."

"Tell me about him."

"He's a widower, a couple of years older than Mom, with two grown kids and three grandkids. He worked in insurance in New Jersey before retiring to Florida."

"His previous wife…."

"Died ten years ago from cancer."

"I'm sorry to hear that."

"He told me he dated a bit before he met Mom, but nothing serious until…."

"Until he met her."

Melody nodded. The spinach was almost done — it smelled divine. "I think you'll like him. He has a big personality. A big laugh. He loves talking."

Barbara stepped closer to inspect the skillet. "The spinach looks perfect."

They heard the back door open and a few seconds later Barbara's husband Stu stepped into the kitchen, overloaded with groceries. He set the bags on the counter with a groan, then turned to Melody. "You made it! Merry Christmas!"

Melody bustled over to give him a hug. He was a

short, round man with a wide grin and a nearly bald head, dressed in blue jeans and a green sweater. "Merry Christmas, Stu. It's so good to see you!"

Melody took a step back and looked at her hosts. The two of them made such a good pair. Such a *great* pair. She felt a pang of longing — she wanted the same for herself — but quickly pushed the thought away. "The spinach is done, so let me help unload the groceries."

"No, dear, you've helped more than enough," Barbara said firmly. "I'll get everything ready in here while Stu helps bring your bags to your room."

"You sure?"

"More than sure," Barbara said. "Dinner in ten. Now scoot!"

CHAPTER 5

*M*elody sighed with satisfaction as she looked around her room. Yes, *her* room. Named the Harvest Room by Barbara and Stu, it was the cozy refuge in which she'd found solace on her first visit to Heartsprings Valley two years earlier, and the room she'd chosen for every visit since. Graciously proportioned, with a king-size bed facing beautiful bay windows, the room breathed autumn, its honey-brown walls blending seamlessly with the auburns and golds and yellows of the furnishings. She ran her hand lovingly over the gorgeous quilt covering the bed — a handmade treasure with a burgundy-red base and an explosion of fall leaves — and gave silent thanks to the universe for allowing her to be here.

Her stomach felt wonderfully full, thanks to Barbara's delicious dinner. Her bags were safely tucked in her room, thanks to Stu. Part of her wanted nothing more than to slip into bed and tumble into dreamland. She had every right to feel exhausted — she'd been going nonstop since breakfast.

But being back in Heartsprings Valley had her eager to experience more. She'd been away too long — she needed a dash of Christmas cheer. The clock on the bedside table told her it was just past eight. Part of her wanted to drive up to her new house and check on the progress. But no, tomorrow was soon enough for that. It would be better to behold the changes to her new home in the bright light of day.

Her fingers lingered on the quilt, the fabric soft to the touch. Barbara had mentioned the stores on the town square staying open late to give folks more time for their Christmas shopping. The square was just a short walk away.

With a smile on her lips, she made up her mind. She'd unpack later. Grabbing her coat, scarf, gloves, and purse, she headed downstairs and spied Stu in the living room, where he was adding an ornament to the Christmas tree.

He glanced over. "Melody, everything okay?"

"Everything's fine. Taking a walk around the square."

"A great night for it. You dressed warm enough?"

"All set."

Stu smiled. "See you in a bit."

"In a bit!"

Her steps brisk, she headed out, passing a lovely old Victorian mansion that now housed the town's animal clinic. Earlier that year, she'd met the veterinarian who ran the clinic — a nice fellow named Nick — at Clara's wedding. His wife Becca, whom Melody already knew, had introduced her to him and their baby daughter, Chloe. She smiled at the memory. They seemed like a wonderful couple and their daughter was adorable. It was nice knowing that, if and when she got a pet, she knew who to turn to for medical attention.

Maybe her musings about future veterinary needs meant she was finally ready for a furry animal companion of her own. Back in New York, with her crazy-busy Broadway schedule, she barely had time to take care of her plants. But up here? She could see herself with a big, confident cat — a charmer who loved sleeping and food and Melody, probably in that order. In her imaginings, her king of the manor would insist on curling up in bed with her, purring softly while she read a lovely book.

Soon. She'd find her charmer soon, once she figured out the next chapter in her life. She picked up her pace, her long legs carrying her effortlessly forward. The night air was cold but not bitterly so. A light breeze brought with it sounds of voices up ahead from the town square.

As she reached her destination, she paused to take in the sight. A light dusting of snow covered the ground. An army of jolly snowmen, snow-women and snow-animals filled the square, welcoming one and all. Brightly colored lights lined the paths to the bandstand in the heart of the square. Every year, a few nights before Christmas, the town's carolers led the community in a sing-along Christmas concert. Two years ago, Melody had been asked to join in and had done so joyously.

A quick glance in both directions confirmed that Barbara was right: Most of the shops lining the square were open late. Shoppers bustled to and fro, loaded with gifts for their loved ones.

She already knew where she truly wanted to be, so she aimed herself in the right direction and got moving. But as she passed the chocolate shop run by her friend Abby, she felt the pull of temptation and stopped to admire the window display. Nestled amidst an arrangement of delicious handmade chocolate treats was a beautiful gingerbread house in the shape of a nineteenth-century farmhouse, clad in clapboard with a big wraparound porch.

In front of the gingerbread house was a gingerbread sign: "Welcome to Northland Orchard." She didn't know the orchard, but she bet it was nearby and that this cookie house was a faithful rendering of the real thing. Behind it stood a row of gingerbread apple trees, along with a card that said, "Courtesy of Becca Shepherd."

A smile came to Melody's lips. She'd forgotten

Becca made gingerbread houses as a hobby. The work was exquisite — so detailed and intricate. The time required had to be staggering. Yet somehow, even with a baby, a husband, and a busy librarian job, Becca had managed to squeeze it in.

Melody's gaze was drawn to the tempting treats displayed in the window. *Was there time for chocolate?* A morsel to tide her over till morning? Her hand moved toward the shop door. *Not now,* she decided, pulling back. If she went in, she'd immediately get lost in gabbing with Abby and end up buying a dozen chocolates, most of which she'd eat as soon as she got back to her room. Tomorrow was the day to see her friend and load up on chocolates for Christmas gifts.

No, tonight was for nourishment of a different sort. Tonight she had a different destination in mind.

She aimed herself toward it, passing Cane Hardware and its big window display. She knew this window well; two years ago, in the course of a busy afternoon, she'd helped Clara, the store owner's daughter, create an impromptu display from scratch.

But this year's display was —

Wow. She paused to take in the sight. *So dazzling!* The window was large, about ten feet across and nearly as tall, and filled with hundreds — maybe thousands — of Christmas ornaments. Each ornament hung individually from the ceiling from a piece of nearly invisible string. Together, they filled the space from ceiling to floor, like a blizzard of ornament snowflakes swirling in the air. Behind them, a lighting system glowed red, green, and white, illuminating the ornaments from behind and creating a sense of movement.

The effect was lush. Breathtaking. A fresh take on a cherished Christmas tradition.

A cold breeze brushed her cheek, reminding her that she was outside on a frigid winter night. Her destination was half a block ahead.

No more distractions. She made a mental note to compliment Clara tomorrow, when they met for breakfast. Ripping her eyes away, she pointed herself toward the real reason she'd emerged from the comfort and warmth of her room at the Inn:

The town's bookstore, The Tattered Page.

Her pace quickened, her spirits rising as she drew nearer. *Once a bookworm, always a bookworm.* Aside from being onstage, there was nothing she loved more than losing herself amongst shelves of books, breathing in their familiar musty smell, running her fingers over titles both familiar and new. How magical to open a book and, in just a few words, leap across time and distance into the imaginings of another, discovering worlds and ideas and characters who surprised and thrilled and moved her. Even as the real world grew faster and more frenetic, a nearby bookstore meant she would always have a place of refuge.

The door's bell chimed as she stepped inside. A rush of warmth greeted her, along with the reassuring scents of books and coffee. Even at this late hour, the place was hopping. Shoppers crowded the display tables near the front, browsing the offerings in search of the perfect gifts for their loved ones. Holiday decorations — a cheerful mix of tinsel and lights — lined the bookshelves and windows.

At the sales counter, a young woman was ringing up purchases as quickly as she could. She had to be tired — the day must have been crazy-busy — but she wasn't showing it. With a big smile and a cheerful "Merry Christmas," she finished with one customer and immediately turned to the next.

As Melody made her way past the register, she heard the young woman say, "Oh, I love this author."

"Isn't she terrific?" the customer replied. "So suspenseful. I buy everything she writes."

Melody slipped past with a smile on her face. The front room of the bookstore was where the new books were displayed, along with shelves filled with nonfiction, biography, cooking, and gardening. But Melody was on the hunt for a good old-fashioned tale, which meant her destination tonight was the annex out back. Unlike the original building, which had been built nearly a century earlier and felt a bit snug, the annex was of recent vintage and consisted of a single large room with a ceiling that rose high above the shelves. It felt like a barn — okay, like what she imagined barns felt like, having little experience with barns herself— but was made with prefab materials. During the day, the space was flooded with natural light from big windows and skylights in the roof. The night ambience was distinctly cozier. Lantern-style sconces along the walls bathed the room in a warm glow. Garlands of tinsel lined the shelves in honor of the holiday. On the far wall was a large, colorful banner boasting a line from Dickens's classic, *A Christmas Carol*: "I will honour Christmas in my heart, and try to keep it all the year."

She felt a tap on her arm and turned to find a young girl, about five or six with shoulder-length brown hair, looking up at her with shy eyes.

"Are you Melody?" the girl asked, a tremor in her voice.

Melody leaned down and gave her a friendly smile. "Yes, darling, I am. What's your name?"

"Julia," the girl said.

"Julia, it's very nice to meet you."

"Do you sing that song?"

Melody chuckled. "Do you mean 'Two Is the Best Number'?" The song, from a Broadway play she'd done several years earlier, was her biggest hit.

Julia's eyes lit up. "Yes!"

"It's one of my favorites."

"My mommy said I should ask."

Melody's gaze moved to a woman standing nearby. "Julia, I'm very glad you did."

The woman joined them. "Ms. Connelly, my name is Nancy."

Melody turned toward her and extended her hand. "Nancy, so nice to meet you. Please, call me Melody."

"My daughter sings your song all the time. I hope it was okay for her to interrupt your browsing."

"Of course," Melody replied. "It's always a pleasure to meet my new neighbors." She turned back to Julia. "Especially when they have wonderful taste in music."

Julia's smile grew bigger. "Are you moving here?"

Melody leaned back down. "I am, darling. I've bought a house and can't wait to move in."

"Do you like books?"

"I love books. How about you?"

The girl glanced up at her mom. "My mommy works here. I can read all the books I want."

"That's marvelous."

Nancy said, "I work here part-time."

"It's a wonderful bookstore."

"Thank you. Anything I can help with?"

"Oh, I'm good. I know right where I'm going." She pointed toward the Mystery section.

Nancy smiled. "We'll let you get to it." She turned to her daughter. "Julia, what do you say to Melody?"

Julia stood up straighter and extended her hand. "Very nice to meet you, Melody."

Melody smiled and took the girl's hand in hers. "Julia, I am so pleased to meet you as well."

Julia flushed, then surprised them all by rushing in and wrapping her arms around Melody's waist for a fierce little hug.

"Oh, my!" Melody said with a laugh.

The girl stepped away, gazing up at her, excitement in her eyes. "Are you really moving here?"

"Yes, darling."

"Forever and always?"

Yes, Melody almost said, but managed to stop herself. What was going on with her? Why that impulse to say *yes*? This town, wonderful though it was, would never be her permanent home. Heartsprings Valley would be her *retreat*. Her second home. Her escape from her real life back in New York.

Right?

"Darling," Melody said, "I'll be spending oodles of time here, promise."

"Are you coming back to the bookstore?"

"Of course."

"Okay," Julia said, apparently satisfied. "Merry Christmas!"

"Merry Christmas, Julia."

"Bye!"

Nancy gave Melody a smile of thanks, then led her daughter away.

Melody watched them go, feeling an unaccustomed glow. Children weren't part of her typical New York existence — most of her friends in the city didn't have them, and the few who did had whisked them off to the suburbs.

This little girl Julia was a sweetheart. Brave, too — clearly nervous about introducing herself, but managing to overcome her shyness and, with her mother's encouragement, stepping forward.

Which is how you learn and grow, she thought. *By taking a chance.*

Smile lingering, she turned toward the Mystery section and happily scanned the offerings, waiting for a book to jump out. As always, one did — an Agatha Christie novel she hadn't read yet, or least didn't remember reading — and she grabbed it.

A wave of exhaustion hit her as she approached the register. It really had been a long day. The Harvest Room and its soft bed beckoned. For a few seconds, as she took in the long line ahead of her, she considered giving up and returning another time.

But the young woman at the register was still cheerful and upbeat, and her day had probably been a lot longer than her own.

Buck up, Melody told herself. *Stay the course.* She watched the young woman ring up book after book with a smile on her face and a kind word for every customer.

Before she knew it, Melody was at the counter and handing over her book. The young woman murmured, "Oh, I love Dame Agatha. Isn't she just the best?"

"Totally agree, darling," Melody said.

The woman glanced up and her eyes widened. "Oh, gosh," she said. "You're Melody Connelly!"

"One and the same. And you are?"

"Anna," the young woman said. "Anna Newcastle." For a second or two, she stared, mouth agog, struggling to find her next words. She was twenty or so, with a round face and a mass of brown hair, wearing big round glasses and a brown sweater.

"I'm sorry," Anna said. "It's just that I'm such a huge fan, Ms. Connelly. I'm the biggest Broadway nerd in New England."

Melody smiled. "Darling, thank you. But please, call me Melody."

"Okay, *Melody*," Anna said with a delighted laugh. "Omigosh. *Melody*. I can't believe this!" Remembering where she was, she gulped and returned her attention to the book. "I didn't know you like mysteries."

"Once a reader, always a reader."

"Me, too. I read everything." A few quick seconds later, with the book rung up and paid for, Anna added, "My dad's part of the team renovating your place on the ridge."

"Oh, is that so?"

"He does woodworking and furniture design. He's been up there all week, restoring moldings and trim and other stuff." She frowned, trying to recall more. "Oh, and he built your new dining table!"

Melody blinked. What had Anna said her last name was? *Newcastle*? "Your father's name is … James Newcastle?"

"That's him."

"He's the artist who built my new custom dining table?"

Anna grinned, pleased. "You seen it yet?"

"Only in photos. I haven't been able to get up here because of my show —"

"— *Manhattan on the Rocks*. Which I saw this summer! I loved it!"

"Thank you — I'm so glad. My contractor has been emailing me a steady stream of updates. I'm heading up tomorrow for my first look in person."

"I hope it's everything you wanted."

"I'm sure it is. The photos of the finished table are gorgeous."

"I'll tell Dad you said so."

"Please do."

Anna glanced at the line. "I should probably…."

"Of course." Melody picked up her new book. "Anna, it's so nice to meet you."

"Same here, Ms. — oops, *Melody*. Thank you so much for coming in tonight. And Merry Christmas!"

Melody looked fondly at the beaming, eager young woman. So much spirit! "Thank you, darling. And Merry Christmas to you!"

CHAPTER 6

The first light of the new day brought Melody a dawning awareness that she had scheduled herself an extremely busy day. Though she'd always been a dreamer and a doer, being an organizer had never been her strong suit. As she reviewed her mental to-do list, she found herself wishing she'd planned a bit more breathing room. Somehow, her day would include:

Having breakfast with Clara and Luke.

Checking out the renovations on her new home.

Shopping, shopping, shopping for Christmas decorations and more.

Being on hand at the Inn to greet her mom and Benny when they arrived.

And so much more!

She rushed through her morning preparations, pulling her hair back into a manageable ponytail and skipping her usual makeup routine. Today was about movement and motion and probably a fair amount of carrying and lifting, so she slipped into worn jeans, t-shirt, sweatshirt, and comfortable winter boots. With a final look in the mirror — Broadway star Melody transformed into woman-on-a-mission Melody — she grabbed her purse and phone and car keys and headed downstairs.

She popped her head into the kitchen, where Barbara and Stu were busy baking. "I'll be out most of the day, darlings."

"You driving up to inspect the house?" Barbara asked.

"After meeting Luke and Clara at the cafe."

"Call if you need anything."

"Will do. Toodles!"

She hopped into her SUV and within minutes was parked outside the Heartsprings Valley Cafe on the town square. The cafe's hand-carved wooden sign, swinging gently in the crisp morning air, was perfect for the season, with "Heartsprings Valley" in cheerful bright red, "Cafe" in creamy white, and fringes of evergreen in the corners.

She pushed open the cafe's wooden door and breathed in the aroma of coffee and fresh-baked treats. Customers were seated at several of the cafe's tables. Warmth from the heating system filled the room, reinforcing the cheerful coziness of the Christmas decorations — the garlands of evergreen bordering the cafe's big windows, the colorful tree ornaments — that seemed to cover every available inch of the walls.

She spied Clara and Luke in line at the counter, a jolt of gladness filling her heart.

They'd seen her, too. Clara rushed up and pulled her in for a hug. "So good to see you, Melody!"

"So glad to be here!"

Reluctantly, Melody let her friend go. Clara was looking her usual energetic self. A tiny slip of a woman in her late twenties, she possessed an aura of calm determination that made her seem larger-than-life. Today she had her shoulder-length brown hair pulled back into a ponytail and was wearing her usual stylish-but-practical combo of jeans, dark-blue sweater, and long black winter coat.

Clara's husband Luke, standing next to her, had a big grin on his handsome face. He was an athletic guy, blond and fit, with startling blue eyes. "Melody," he said. "Great to see you." As usual, he was dressed like the general contractor he was: jeans and flannel shirt, with a work belt around his waist and an ever-present clipboard in his hand.

Melody gave him a brief hug. "So how are you two newlyweds?"

"We're great," Clara said.

The diamond in Clara's wedding ring sparkled in the morning light. The two of them looked so good together. Their wedding — so lovely — had taken place that spring in front of a white gazebo over-looking Heartsprings Lake. The happy couple, home-town kids who'd traveled the world before returning home, knew how lucky they were to have found each other. Clara had been radiant, Luke emotional, their families and friends joyful.

Melody felt her throat catch as she remembered the day. At the reception, she'd been honored to perform a song — "At Last" — to accompany their first dance as a married couple.

"What can we order for you?" Luke asked.

"Mmm, something decadent, darling," Melody replied. "A mocha latte would be perfect."

"Have you had the scones here?" Clara asked. "Baked fresh every day, and soooo good."

Melody scanned the options in the display case. "Twist my arm. Cranberry-apple sounds perfect."

Coffees and scones in hand, they found a table near the window and got to catching up on the various goings-on in their lives since they'd seen each other last — Melody telling them about her latest show, Clara and Luke about their first months of married life. Outside, the morning sun reflected brightly on the snowpeople dotting the town square.

Luke opened his clipboard. "I know what you're really interested in."

Melody smiled. "You have no idea."

"You must be excited to see everything in person."

"Bursting!"

He chuckled. "It definitely feels good to be in the home stretch."

Item by item, he took her through the recent work his crew had completed. The big jobs — heating, ventilation, gas, electric, water, lighting, flooring — were finished.

"The kitchen and bathrooms are almost done," he said. "A few touches left. The fireplace is done — we installed the mantel yesterday."

"So I can sit by my roaring fire with a cup of hot cocoa and get toasty warm?" she asked.

"Absolutely."

"And you said the kitchen's almost done, too?"

"Nearly. Countertop, appliances, even the cabinet knobs. The new fridge went in yesterday."

"Wonderful. What's still on the list?"

"A lot of trim work. I've got a guy — really talented craftsman — doing most of it. He's set up a temporary woodworking shop in the media room. He's working up there today, so you'll meet him."

"And what else is left?"

"You have decorating choices to make upstairs — paint colors, wallpaper selections, a couple of other things. I left a list and a bunch of samples for you to review."

Melody felt a rush of pleasure. Her dream home was becoming more real by the second.

"And what else?"

"Well," he said, scanning his notes, "aside from the dining table and the two big matching sofas for the living area, you don't have any furniture yet."

"That's on schedule for tomorrow?"

He nodded. "Tomorrow's the day. Big trucks can't do Summit Lane in the winter, so we're loading everything onto smaller trucks. We'll do runs all day until we get everything up there."

Clara, who had been listening quietly, touched Luke's arm. "If the weather cooperates."

"The weather?" Melody said with a frown. She glanced outside at the clear blue sky.

"A storm's headed our way," Luke said. "Due this afternoon. If we're lucky, it'll be snow."

Melody felt an anxious jolt. "And if we're not lucky?"

Luke shrugged. "They're saying it could be ice."

"An ice storm?"

"Depends on the temperature."

Melody tried to stay calm. Ice storms were probably a regular part of living here, after all. "What if it's an ice storm?"

"Ice is heavier than snow. If it's ice, we'll most likely see tree branches and power lines come down."

"And if that happens?"

He gave her a reassuring smile. "We'll get through it, just as we always do."

Clara jumped in. "The town has the right trucks

and equipment to clear the roads. If we get hit, we'll be out from under in no time."

"Oh, gosh," Melody said, momentarily at a loss for words.

Clara reached out and squeezed her hand. "Welcome to Heartsprings Valley. Land of the occasional ice storm."

"Hitting this afternoon, you said?"

Luke nodded. "That's what the meteorologists are saying."

"Okay," Melody said, her mind racing. She had so much to do today — how was she going to get everything done?

Then she realized, with a jolt:

Her mom and Benny!

"I should call my mom," Melody said. "She and her husband are driving up this afternoon."

While Clara and Luke watched, Melody hit the "Mom" button on her phone.

After a few rings, she heard her mom's voice. "Morning, dear!"

"Morning, mom!" Melody said. "How are you and Benny? Have you landed in New York yet?"

"Fine, dear. I was about to call. We just got off our flight. We're at the rental car agency. Benny's getting our SUV."

"Oh, good. So you'll be on the road soon?"

"That's right, dear. Everything okay?"

"Everything's fine, but I just found out we're due for a storm this afternoon."

"Oh, my."

"It'll probably arrive around the same time as you."

"Benny's a good driver. We'll be fine."

"I'm sure you're right. But don't dilly-dally, okay? I want you safe and sound at the Inn before the storm arrives."

"I'll give you a call with our ETA when we're on the road."

"Okay, mom. Love you."

"Love you, too. Talk to you soon!"

Melody slipped her phone back into her pocket and found two pairs of concerned eyes looking at her.

"How's your mom?" Clara asked.

"She's fine," Melody said, then explained their travel plans. "She'll be okay driving up, right?"

Luke nodded. "Oh, sure. The main road into town is always the first priority. It's salted and kept in good shape. Did they get a four-wheel drive?"

Melody nodded.

"Then they should be fine."

"Okay," she replied, exhaling anxiously. "Now I'm wishing I'd stayed in New York yesterday. I could have driven up with them."

"Well," Clara said, reasonable as always, "there's no point in worrying about something you can't change." She rubbed her hands together. "I assume you have errands today?"

"I do," Melody said.

"Let's hear 'em. I can help."

"You don't have to do that."

Clara gave her a patient smile. "Of course I do. I'm your friend. And I'm good at this kind of stuff."

Melody grinned. Oh, she'd missed Clara so much! When it came to organizing, no one was better. "Darling, you are a treasure beyond words. You sure I'm not getting in the way of your duties as town manager?"

"As town manager," Clara replied, "it's my job to make sure our new residents are welcomed with open arms."

Which was true enough, Melody supposed. Clara's job probably really did encompass all manner of civic responsibilities. But still....

"You must have things to do to get ready for the storm."

"Nothing I can't handle with this," Clara said, pointing to her phone. She turned to her husband. "Were you planning to go up to the house with Melody?"

"I was planning to...." he began.

"But now you're thinking about the storm and how it might be better to focus on getting everything prepped for tomorrow's move-in before the storm hits."

He smiled lovingly at her. "I married a mind reader."

Clara smiled back playfully. "You deal with the organizing. I'll drive up with Melody."

"You sure?"

When she nodded, he leaned over and gave her cheek a kiss.

"That okay with you?" he said to Melody.

"More than okay, darling. But you two have to stop being so adorable."

Clara laughed, Luke grinned, and for a few seconds, Melody's anxiety about the storm vanished.

"Okay," Luke said, standing up. "We should get going. Lots to do."

They grabbed their things, but as they headed toward the door, a woman stepped from behind the counter carrying a cardboard box emblazoned with the "Heartsprings Valley Cafe" logo.

"Hey, guys, hold on!" the woman said.

Melody had met the woman before — she'd been a bridesmaid at Clara's wedding. *What was her name again?* Late thirties, a lovely face, shoulder-length brown hair, warm and friendly. At the wedding, she'd had a man on her arm, a handsome fellow who ran an apple orchard....

The name came. "Holly?" Melody said.

"Melody, so good to see you," Holly said. "Welcome back."

"Thank you." More memories came: Holly was

the owner of this very cafe. But something about her was different….

"I have something for you," Holly said. "A welcome gift."

Melody blinked with surprise. "For me? You didn't have to do that."

Holly handed her the box. "It's a sampler. One of every kind of scone and muffin we bake."

"You're too kind. I couldn't possibly accept this."

Holly shook her head, her eyes twinkling. "Sorry, no choice!"

Melody's attention was drawn to a sparkle on the ring of the third finger of Holly's left hand. The sparkle hadn't been there that spring, because the ring hadn't been there that spring. Melody made a mental note to get the scoop from Clara.

"Holly, thank you so much," Melody said. "I'm sure I'm going to love each and every one of these treats."

"I know you have a busy day," Holly said, "so I'll let you get to it."

"I'm sure I'll see you very soon," Melody said.

"Counting on it. See you soon!"

CHAPTER 7

$\mathcal{M}$oments later, her hands gripping the wheel of her SUV, Melody headed out of town, Clara in the passenger seat next to her. They made their way across the valley. The sky was still clear and blue, the sun still bright.

"I can't believe I'm about to see my new home," Melody confessed. "After all these months away, it still feels like a dream."

"A dream built on lots of hard work," Clara said. "The ridge road is up ahead."

"On the left?"

"You remembered."

"There are only so many choices out here."

Clara laughed. "So true."

Melody turned onto the ridge road and almost immediately began to climb. Stands of tall evergreens, lightly dusted with snow, rose on either side of them. The road, a series of switchbacks, rose gradually at first, then with increasing steepness, the turns becoming sharper and more pronounced.

"You and Luke seem happy," Melody said as she skillfully took a curve.

"We are."

"How's his contracting business?"

"Great. He had a busy fall." She briefly recounted the projects he was working on, including Melody's house.

"And you?" Melody asked. "You keeping busy, too?"

"Of course. Which is good. Busy's good. We both like being busy."

Melody remembered what she'd noticed at the cafe. "Was that a ring on Holly's finger?"

Clara nodded. "She and Gabe got engaged a few weeks ago. After the harvest season finally quieted down, he proposed and whisked her away for a romantic weekend."

"How lovely. I'm happy for her."

"Me, too. They're good for each other. Two busy entrepreneurs who understand and support each other." She glanced over at Melody. "How about you?"

"Me?"

"Dating anyone?"

Melody shook her head, trying to ignore the pang of regret. "A few first dates, but...."

"No one you hit it off with?"

"Not much chance of that," Melody replied, perhaps a bit too briskly. "Not with the show demanding every waking moment."

Clara gave her a sympathetic nod and her phone buzzed. She read the message and frowned. "Sorry, have to answer this."

"No worries." For the next couple of minutes, while Clara typed away, Melody turned her attention to the beauty surrounding her. The trees were older and taller up here. Nature seemed bigger and closer. Through occasional gaps, she caught sight of the valley far below.

For reasons she couldn't begin to fathom, her thoughts jumped to Anna, the young woman she'd met at the bookstore the previous night. After leaving the bookstore and returning to the Inn, Melody had powered up her laptop and rooted through her email until she found the photos that Luke had sent of her new custom dining table. Made from reclaimed cedar, the table was as gorgeous as she'd remembered.

Clearly, the man who made the table — Anna's father — was a talented craftsman. Curious to learn more, she'd clicked over to his website and found a portfolio of his custom work, with beautiful photos of wood cabinets, shelving, dining tables, and more. The contact page included a brief bio: "James

Newcastle lives in Heartsprings Valley with his daughter Anna."

As bios went, it was short — way too short. Vexingly incomplete. She wanted to know more, starting with: What did he look like?

"You're frowning," Clara said.

With a jolt, Melody snapped back. "I am?"

"What's on your mind?"

"Nothing, darling, nothing." Then, without warning, she found herself saying, "Though I did run into Derek yesterday."

Clara sat up, instantly alert, fully aware of all the implications. "Really? Where?"

Melody gave her a rundown of their encounter, then gestured toward a side road up ahead. "The next right?"

"Yes," Clara said with barely a glance, her attention laser-focused on the Derek news. "What was it like, seeing him? And hearing him say what he said?"

Melody turned onto her new road, Summit Lane. "Honestly, I'm not sure." She slowed a bit as she adjusted to the road, which was narrower and twistier than the ridge road. There were homes up here, but they were fewer and farther between — outposts of domesticity amidst a thick forest of pines.

"Not sure in what way?" Clara replied carefully.

"I suppose I'm not sure because...." Melody paused, her voice trailing off.

Then, with a sudden rush:

"Because I haven't forgotten how much it hurt when he dumped me."

As the words left her mouth, Melody realized she was glad she'd said them. The truth stung sometimes, but it could also be freeing.

"Well," Clara said loyally, "I've been boycotting his movies ever since."

Melody let out a surprised laugh. "Tell me you haven't done that."

"Oh, but I have," Clara said firmly. "I was very disappointed in him. Still am." She pointed to a bend ahead. "Your place is coming up a bit after the bend."

Melody felt her anticipation rising. Her new house was barely a minute away!

"Of course," Clara said, "I suppose I should be open to forgiving him and moving on — as long as you are, of course. I'm glad he admitted he screwed up."

Melody looked at her friend with affection. Clara had been this way from the instant she'd met her: Firm in her convictions, clear in her actions, and practical and open-minded when it came to moving forward.

"You're going to make a great mayor someday."

Clara waved the idea away. "Oh, stop."

"Isn't Mayor Winters constantly threatening to retire?"

"Constantly. But it'll never happen. He loves this town too much. Which is fine with me. He's a dream boss."

"And the job?"

"Wouldn't trade it for anything. Besides, I might have other priorities the next few years."

"Oh, is that so?" Melody with a big grin, knowing exactly what Clara was referring to. "Is there something to report?"

"No, no, no, not yet," Clara said, flushing pink. "But maybe, hopefully, sometime in the next year."

"Well, I wish you and Luke the best of luck."

"Thank you."

Melody gave her friend a fond glance. Clara seemed irritated with herself, probably because she hadn't planned to say anything about her near-term plans. And yet she had.

Time to change the subject. Melody gestured toward the forest surrounding them. "I'm surprised there isn't much snow yet."

"It's been light so far, but it'll come. Just you wait."

"Wait?" Melody shook her head and sat up straighter. "Oh, no — no more waiting, darling. I'm officially done with waiting. The time for waiting has passed."

Clara smiled. "I sense a pronouncement."

Melody laughed. "A proclamation. A promise. A declaration. Henceforth, I ban the cursed word 'waiting' from my vocabulary."

"No more waiting?"

"Not even for a second! Darling, I'm positively bursting to see my new home!"

Clara smiled. "Then let the bursting commence."

Ahead of them, Summit Lane ended at a gravel driveway, next to a shiny new red mailbox with the number "1" on it.

Melody brought the SUV to a stop as a wave of anticipation rushed through her.

"Darling," she said exultantly, "I'm home!"

CHAPTER 8

For just a second, as she gazed upon her shiny new mailbox, Melody flashed back to the autumn day more than a year earlier when she'd first arrived at this very spot. Clara had been with her that day, too, tagging along as Melody searched for "a retreat, darling, from the hustle and bustle of New York."

Their day had been a busy one, and a frustrating one. They'd seen five properties, none of them right. And with the afternoon sun beginning its descent, they knew the day wouldn't be with them much longer.

Hopes fading, they'd reached the end of a winding road called Summit Lane near the top of Heartsprings Ridge. Clara consulted her list of available properties, then pointed to a lonely, rusty mailbox with the number "1" on it, standing forlornly next to a gravel driveway. "This must be it."

Melody turned into the driveway, which looked uneven and in dire need of upkeep. Tires crunching on the rough surface, they followed the path through a stand of old-growth pine trees.

"Tell me again what you want?" Clara asked, trying as always to be helpful.

"Beauty and warmth and connection," Melody replied.

"I was thinking more about how many bedrooms and bathrooms."

"Oh, lots."

"And what kind of style?"

"Oh, lots of style, too."

Clara gave her a look. "You don't know what you want, do you?"

"Darling," Melody replied, "I'll know it the instant I see it."

The afternoon sun filtered through the trees, dappling the ground in light and shadow. There was beauty here, but also rawness. Nature up here was bolder, more vivid. The town, just a short drive down the ridge, seemed very far away.

"Have you been to this property before?" Melody asked.

"Never. The trees are lovely."

"Yes, lovely."

"But this driveway is another story."

Carefully, Melody eased past a spot where erosion had worn half the gravel away. "What do we know about this place?"

"Five acres. Unoccupied. The owners retired to Florida years ago and have been trying to sell it ever since."

"Which explains the condition of the road."

The path emerged from the trees and took them across an open meadow, wild and overgrown with tall grasses.

And then, at the far side of the meadow —

Melody inhaled, seized immediately by a rush of impressions and feelings.

A house rose before them, silent and alone.

It was Victorian in appearance, with the distinctive gables and moldings and adornments of houses of that era. It was a substantial structure — two full stories plus an attic, with a tall tower that rose even higher. Its once-white paint had faded to a neglected, dirty grey.

"Oh my," Clara said as they slowly approached.

"Oh my is right," Melody breathed, her gaze roving over the intricate exterior details. She brought the car to a halt and stared up at a house that now seemed to loom over them.

Her heart was thumping as a rush of emotions surged through her.

Her gut was talking to her. No, not talking — shouting. Telling her what she already knew:

She'd lucked upon something unusual.

Something gripping.

Something rare and special.

Without a doubt, there was something *magical* about this grand but faded Victorian house on the meadow at the top of the ridge.

"Let's take a look," Clara said, her tone wary and resigned, clearly not seeing or feeling the same.

Afraid to break the spell, Melody unbuckled her seat belt, turned off the engine, and stepped outside. The autumn air retained a fragile warmth from the late-afternoon sun. A soft breeze carried hints of dried grass and fallen leaves.

Briefly, as she turned her gaze upward, a glimmer of uncertainty rippled through her. For a split second, she saw what Clara saw: A building in desperate need of repair. An old house suffering from years, perhaps decades, of neglect.

Calling it "rough" would be an understatement.

Calling it a "teardown" was perhaps stating the inevitable.

But rushing to that conclusion would be unfair, she somehow knew. Something about this house *resonated*. Something about its profile, which seemed so proud and stately, standing watch from its place at the edge of the meadow. It seemed patient, even stoic. Like it was waiting for the right person to show up and make it whole again.

Like it knew what it took to persevere.

To *survive.*

"It's perfect," Melody said, unable to hold back an instant longer, her eyes shining as excitement flooded through her.

Clara turned toward her, gaping with astonishment. "*What?*"

"I'll fix it up. Restore it."

"This pile?"

"Yes, darling," Melody said.

"*Really?*"

"Really."

"But you haven't even been inside!"

"I hear it calling me."

"You mean you hear it begging to be torn down and put out of its misery?"

Melody laughed. "Oh, stop. Such beautiful bones. Don't you see? I have the most wonderful feeling. This house is going to be just grand."

"Grandly expensive," Clara said, unwilling to budge.

"Grandly gorgeous."

"Grandly troublesome."

"Nonsense." A thought came. "Perhaps Luke can swing by and poke around?"

Clara frowned. "He could do that," she said slowly. "And if he tells you to run?"

"Then I'll scamper, darling. I'll dash as fast as I can."

Clara returned her gaze to the house, apparently

debating whether to continue objecting. Then, as if accepting defeat, she let out a sigh. "You're just a little bit crazy, you know that? I say that with respect and affection."

Melody laughed. "Do we have the keys? I desperately want to get inside."

Clara nodded, then pointed to a stone path that led around the side of the house. "Let's walk around the outside first."

Together, they followed the stone path to the back of the house. As they rounded the bend, they saw a big covered porch that ran along the rear.

And beyond that —

This time, they both gasped.

"Oh, my," Clara said softly.

Behind the house, below them in the distance, lay a sweeping, panoramic view of the valley and Heart-springs Lake, shimmering in the afternoon sun. The vista was unexpected, breathtaking, dramatic.

For a long moment, stunned into silence, all they could do was take it in.

"Look," Clara said, pointing. "You can see the town square."

"And the Inn," Melody added, gesturing to a white dot a block away.

"I had no idea this view even existed."

"Just think, darling — once this place is fixed up, you'll be able to come over and enjoy it whenever you want."

A hint of a smile came to Clara's lips. Melody could see the gears in her friend's ever-practical head starting to turn.

"Okay," Clara finally said. "I'm seeing how this might work. *Maybe.*"

"I'm so glad, darling."

"I said *maybe.*"

"Of course."

"I'll have Luke come over here and kick the tires."

"Thank you."

"But if he gives you bad news —"

"Then I move on."

"Promise?"

"Promise, darling."

Clara exhaled. "Fine." She held up the key. "Then let's get inside and check this place out."

Melody blinked at the memory of that magical first visit. A wave of excitement rose within her as she realized:

Her new home was ready for its debut!

Oh, how long she'd been waiting (oh, cursed word) for this moment. Over a year of work and time and money. So much planning and waiting and adjusting and more waiting. So many emails and phone calls and decisions.

All sparked by a dream — her dream — for this

house on the hill to be reborn. From an early age, she'd always been a dreamer. And though her visions didn't always come to fruition, sometimes, more often that she had any right to expect, they did.

It was a lesson she'd been fortunate to learn early in life. A lesson whose teachings she never stopped applying, in ways large and small:

Share your dreams with the universe. Shout them out loud, with joy in your heart. Because the universe might be listening.

As promised, Clara had corralled Luke into checking out the place. When he'd reported back — with reluctance — that the house was not a complete and total disaster, but rather just *mostly* a disaster, Melody had immediately hired her New York friend Teddy as project architect and persuaded Luke to join the team as general contractor. Together, the three of them had come up with a plan that thrilled her:

Carefully restoring the home's entry hall, living room, library, and dining room.

Modernizing the kitchen.

Updating the bathrooms throughout.

Turning the unfinished basement into a modern media room.

Transforming the attic into a new master suite.

And, last but not least, cosmetic updates and repairs for the second-floor bedrooms.

There had been moments — too many — when

the house came close to defeating them. Luke had warned her the house needed a new roof, new windows, new electrical, new heating, new ventilation, and repairs galore for cracked plaster and damaged wood floors. Inevitably, as the renovation progressed, more problems were unearthed: Ancient plumbing. A crumbling foundation. Water damage. Rot and mold and termites and more.

At times, the list of repairs seemed to extend into infinity.

Through it all, she'd remained steadfast: Her stoic, stately house on the hill would be reborn. It deserved the care and attention she was lavishing upon it. It didn't matter that Teddy and Luke thought her unrealistic at times — she got that response whenever she expressed big dreams out loud.

In the passenger seat next to her, Clara said, "You ready?"

Melody swallowed. She pressed the pedal and turned onto the gravel driveway. The path beneath them was solid and firm now — fully repaired and restored. The SUV moved smoothly through the trees.

By silent agreement, neither of them spoke. They emerged from the woods onto the meadow, which had been trimmed back but otherwise left alone. Come spring, Melody would have decisions to make about what to do with the space. She liked the idea of keeping it wild and natural, but adding a small patio nestled beneath a pergola, where she could relax with her morning latte and a good book....

All thoughts of future landscape design faded away as her new home came into view.

Her mouth fell open. Tears came as her emotions threatened to overwhelm her.

Her new home was — oh, my — *gorgeous*. It was crisply white now, gleaming brightly in the morning sun, its original grandeur proudly restored. With its turrets and spires and shingles and moldings and decorative elements she couldn't even begin to guess the names of, it seemed like something out of a dream — a Hollywood version of a Victorian fantasy. Yet somehow, despite ornaments and details that bordered on the theatrical, her new home retained its aura of stately dignity.

They pulled to a stop in front. Barely able to contain herself, Melody ripped off her seat belt and leaped out of the SUV.

"Oh, darling," she said, her voice barely a whisper, "my baby is *back*."

Clara joined her outside. "Look at the tower," she said, pointing upward to the column rising four stories into the sky. "Luke put in the new weathervane just yesterday."

Melody ran her eyes upward and landed on the gleaming copper rooster. At that moment, the wind shifted and the rooster swung westward. For the first time, she noticed a decorative roof element circling the rooster vane, a ring of shingles shaped like sunflower petals. She was going to have to learn the names for all these decorations, she realized, because how else was going to be able to tell people how wonderful her new house was?

"I have to get inside," she said.

Clara smiled. "After you."

Together, they dashed up the stairs to the porch. At the front door — the original oak front door, now restored and stained a rich brown — Clara handed Melody a key.

"Here you go, homeowner."

Melody's hand trembled. The key looked and felt completely ordinary — a small piece of metal, nearly identical to millions of others — yet it represented something important and meaningful. This little piece of metal meant she was entering a new chapter in her life. A step worth noting, honoring, and remembering.

She slipped the key into the lock, then turned it, the bolt sliding with a soft click. With her other hand, she gripped the handle, pushed open the door and —

Walked into her new home.

CHAPTER 9

A year earlier, soon after buying the place, Melody had done some reading on Victorian homes in New England and learned that a grand entry hall — like the one in her new home — was typical of large houses of the period. Her entry hall hadn't been much to look at when she'd first laid eyes on it. Buried beneath years of neglect and grime, it had seemed sad and empty.

But now — *wow*. Again came tears. She loved when dreams came true. Her restored entry hall positively *gleamed*. The original wood wall paneling had been brought back to life meticulously, the natural beauty of the wood enhanced by a honey-colored stain and polish.

Clara pressed a light switch next to the door. An ornate crystal chandelier, rewired for the twenty-first century, bathed the entry hall in a warm glow.

Melody gasped as she drank in the sight of her restored staircase. *So grand!* Rushing forward, she gripped the ornate banister's rounded knob. The steps, now clad in a rich red carpet runner, seemed to beckon her upward.

"It's so beautiful," she said, whirling toward Clara.

Clara blushed, clearly pleased that her friend — and husband's client — was thrilled. "I wish Luke had been here for the big reveal."

"Oh, me, too. Can you imagine, once the furniture is here? This place will be divine!" She grabbed her friend by the arm. "I want to start at the very top."

Clara grinned. "Lead the way."

Together, they rushed up the stairs to the second floor — devoted to bedrooms — and then up a smaller set of stairs to the attic. Having settled on her plan of attack, Melody didn't allow herself to be distracted, though part of her wanted to linger and gawk and poke at every single detail. Instead, with Clara in tow, she made her way to the winding metal stairs that led up into the home's tower.

A tower in a home felt so unnecessary, in a way — an indulgence and an extravagance. Which perhaps explained why she loved it so much. Due to roof leaks and water damage, the tower hadn't been safe to climb when she'd bought the place. It was only after structural fixes and installation of a new staircase that she'd been able to explore it. As a result, she'd only been up it once, during her last visit back in the spring.

Barely able to contain her excitement, she gripped the railing of the new spiral metal staircase and made her way up. The stairs rose two stories through the center of the tower, like a dramatic black sculpture. The surrounding walls, painted a bright white and almost close enough to be touched, would soon host artwork and photos and all manner of mementos.

The stairs led to an open room at the top of the tower. Originally, the space had been the equivalent of a covered patio, open to the elements. But now, at Melody's behest, the space had been enclosed. New windows offered views on all sides. Radiant heat installed in the floors and walls ensured the room would be cozy on even the coldest of nights. It wasn't a large space, but she already knew exactly how it would be furnished, with a love seat facing the view of the town and oodles of potted plants to drink up the sun. Bathed in bright morning light, the room already seemed so warm and welcoming.

Clara turned toward Heartsprings Lake, which sparkled in the distance. "I'm so glad you closed this room in. I could look at this view forever."

"I want you to come over anytime you need a fix."

Clara's phone buzzed, and she glanced down and frowned. "You'd think life in a small town would be slower and easier than in New York. That is *so* not the case." She sighed and got to typing.

"What's going on?"

"Just some confusion about who borrowed an electric saw. We need it for road clearing."

"For the ice storm?"

Clara heard the hint of anxiety in Melody's voice and looked up. "No need for you to worry. Everything will be fine."

Melody glanced at the skies, which were still blue and clear. "It sure doesn't look like a storm is coming."

Clara pointed toward the lake. "It'll hit us from the east, from across the lake. But not for another few hours."

"Let's keep exploring."

Clara nodded. "After you."

They made their way down the winding staircase to the attic, which would soon be Melody's master suite. It was a large, airy, open space, painted white. The sloping walls and window placements created angles and nooks and crannies that Melody found delightful, the morning sun casting light and shadows that seemed to change by the second. Figuring out how to decorate the suite would be a challenge — one she couldn't wait to tackle.

Clara looked around the open area. "Where will the bed go?"

"I'm planning to put it there," Melody said,

pointing to a gently sloping wall between two windows.

Clara nodded. "Let's check out the bathroom."

Eagerly, Melody made her way past her new walk-in closet into her new bathroom. She'd spent so much time that summer scouring the Internet for just the right tiles and fixtures as she, Teddy, and Luke debated the designs for the bathrooms and kitchen. The direction they chose was clear — fully modern with a traditional look — but the options and possibilities had been bewildering.

Still, they'd persevered. And though she'd seen photos of the completed room already, she couldn't help but gasp as she gazed in person upon the results of their combined labors.

Her new master bathroom was *dazzling*. So bright and cheery, with morning light from the big bay window reflecting off the crisp white subway tiles (accented with black-and-grey) that she'd chosen as the room's primary color scheme. The clawfoot tub beneath the window — original to the house and now fully restored — gleamed in the sun, its chrome fixtures sparkling like silver jewels. The walk-in shower, side-by-side sinks, and built-in storage offered everything a city girl could dream of.

"I love this bathroom," Clara said.

"So do I."

"I could move in and never leave."

Melody laughed.

"Seriously," Clara continued. "I'll just camp out in the tub and spend my days blissed out in a never-ending bubble bath, with nothing but a good book and a glass of wine and my phone somewhere far, far away...."

Melody laughed again. "Anytime you want, this bathroom is yours. My refuge is your refuge."

Clara gestured to the empty walls above the sinks. "No mirrors or vanity cabinets yet, I see."

"I'm sure those will be here soon." Melody turned on a sink faucet and ran her hand under the water. Within seconds, it was warm and then hot. "Oh, darling, this is marvelous. An actual, honest-to-goodness, functioning water heater."

Clara laughed. "Unlike New York?"

"I love my apartment to death, but the water takes forever to warm up."

"New plumbing and heating — gotta love it."

At that moment, Melody felt her phone vibrate. She reached into her coat and pulled it out.

Her mom had texted a message: "New York behind us. There around five. Can't wait to see you!"

"Can't wait!" Melody texted back. "Drive safely. Let me know when you're close!"

"Who's that?" Clara asked.

"My mom," Melody replied. "She and Benny will get here around five."

"We should keep exploring."

"Absolutely." With a final lingering glance,

Melody followed Clara down to the second floor. Quickly, they peeked into the floor's new bathroom (also gorgeous) before moving on to the bedrooms. Aside from new heating and electrical, the renovations in the bedrooms had been mostly cosmetic — wood floors refinished, plaster cracks filled in, trim and moldings repaired.

Which meant the bedrooms were now ready for final decorating decisions. In the largest of the three bedrooms, Melody found a work table with a big stack of wallpaper samples, along with a note from Luke that said: "Take a look and let me know what you think."

Melody picked up a sample of burgundy wallpaper — rich and glamorous and oozing luxury — and held it up. "Hmmm," she said, turning to Clara. "What say you?"

Clara shook her head. "Too powerful and intense for a large room or wall. But I could see it working well in a powder room."

"Agree." Quickly, she flipped through the options, pausing occasionally before moving to the next. She'd selected most of the samples herself, but none was really jumping out and grabbing her — until, near the bottom of the stack, she reached a design that gave her pause. It was a creamy linen wallpaper with a cloth texture, decorated with a hand-painted line drawing of an evergreen forest. The effect was elegant and subtle, the mood almost dreamy.

"Oh, that's nice," Clara said. "You could use that anywhere. Maybe in the hallway?"

"Yes," Melody said, setting it aside. "Definitely a leading contender."

At that moment, Clara's phone buzzed again. She glanced at it and frowned. "Sorry, need to…."

"No worries, darling," Melody said. "I'll head downstairs and keep exploring."

Clara nodded. "Join you in a bit."

CHAPTER 10

*M*elody couldn't keep the smile off her face as she made her way down the stairs. To have these beautiful rooms brought back to life, shining and glowing once again....

Excitement flooded through her as she realized she'd barely seen half of what her new home had to offer. The lion's share of the restoration had taken place on the ground floor, and she had yet to lay eyes on her new kitchen, dining room, powder room, study, and living room.

Where to begin? She nearly laughed out loud: It didn't matter!

"Kitchen," she announced to herself. "Definitely the kitchen."

She walked down the entry hall, stopping briefly to peek at her new powder room (lovely!) before pushing through the swinging door at the end of the hall into the kitchen that she intended to start putting to very good use very soon. She wasn't an expert cook or baker — her mom had done most of the cooking growing up, and during her years in New York she simply hadn't had the time — but all of that was going to change.

And it was going to change right here, in the renovated space her eyes now roamed over, feasting on every detail. She and Teddy and Luke had gone a bit gaga over the planning for the room, tossing ideas back and forth, researching new options, adding adjustments and tweaks — until Melody, unable to bear even one more moment of indecision, had put her foot down and said, "Guys, this is it. My dream kitchen. Let's do it."

In the end, their plan hewed closely to the kitchen's original design, with modern updates to bring the space into the twenty-first century. The primary color palette was creamy white, with tile work and painted cabinets whose soft tones allowed the modern appliances to pop. At one end of the large room was the kitchen's visual anchor, a huge fireplace and chimney, with a hearth nearly six feet wide and several feet deep, now decorated in lovely mocha tiles. Back in the nineteenth century, before the house included an oven, the hearth had been a walk-in affair, where the cooks could keep multiple pots boiling over multiple small fires. Now it housed a meticulously restored gas oven that seemed to beckon her toward it, as if begging for her to start using it.

With a surge of optimism, she envisioned herself cooking a lovely ham, baking cookies and cakes, stirring up delicious hot chocolate....

She chuckled as a thought came: Nigel would be so distressed if he knew how domestic she intended to become! He wanted her focused on her next big gig — the role that would push her career to even greater heights. If he discovered that what she cared about most right now was making her new home a warm and welcoming place, the poor man would throw a fit.

She walked along the lovely wall of cabinets and counters that offered more storage than she'd ever need, her fingers trailing across her new white marble countertops. Teddy and Luke had recommended a different material — something less prone to wear and tear — but Melody had insisted on staying natural. She wanted to see and feel the nicks and dents, the cracks and stains, that were certain to appear over time. Each imperfection, she hoped, would bring forth a memory and bear witness to the history she intended to establish.

The center of the room was for a large wooden farm table, due to be delivered the following day. She walked to her new refrigerator — gorgeous, gleaming stainless steel — and opened it, nodding with satisfaction, then ran her eyes over the farm-house sink, wine refrigerator, and dishwasher.

Yes, everything looked great. Just as she'd imagined. Though it was jarring how empty the cabinets and fridge were. She'd have to address that when she went shopping. It would be good to have a few of the basics — coffee, tea, hot chocolate, assorted snacks and treats — to offer Luke's crew when they moved everything in.

She remembered: Holly's treats were still in her SUV! She pivoted toward the kitchen's back door and went down the side steps to the stone path that ran along the side of the house. At the SUV, after grabbing the box of scones from her back seat, she paused to gaze up again at her restored beauty of a home, tears welling in amazement at the transformation.

"You did good, girl," she said out loud. A gust of wind whipped across the open field, reminding her that there was much to do and not nearly enough time in the day to do it.

She hurried to the front door and once again felt a small thrill as she slid the key into the lock and stepped inside. Making her way back to the kitchen, she set the box of scones on the counter and was about to continue exploring when she heard a faint sound.

A muffled sound, but distinct nonetheless.

A high-pitched whir — like a machine had been turned on.

And then, just as suddenly, the sound stopped.

Melody froze, puzzled. What was Clara up to?

But just as quickly, she dismissed that line of thinking. The sound was from a machine, and Clara didn't have any machines with her.

A thought came: Should she be alarmed?

CHAPTER 11

*S*ilent and still, Melody tried to suss out the source of the unexplained noise. For a few long seconds, her mind racing, she tried to identify what kind of sound it was and who or what could be making it.

Then, with a rush of relief, she remembered: Luke had said a woodworking specialist would be on site today.

And then more dots connected. Anna, the young woman at the bookstore, had said her dad — the woodworking craftsman who had built her new dining table — was part of the renovation team.

Which very likely meant Anna's dad was here doing work somewhere in this big house, right at this very moment.

The high-pitched whir started up again. Eager to

confirm her speculations, she left the kitchen and made her way toward the sound.

At the head of the stairs leading down to the basement level, she heard the machine whir again and caught the familiar scent of sawdust.

The sound was coming from her new media room. With curiosity and a hint of anxiety, she made her way down.

Her gaze landed on a man — presumably the craftsman, James Newcastle — at a large work table set up in the middle of the room. His back was toward her. He was wearing ear muffs and safety glasses and was dressed in work boots, jeans, and a red-and-black flannel shirt.

He hadn't heard or noticed her, his full attention on a small piece of wood he was carefully positioning beneath a circular saw.

She was about to step closer to introduce herself but found herself holding back.

She wanted to see how he approached his task, she told herself. He seemed utterly focused, as if nothing mattered more than the cut he was about to make. He made a final adjustment, turned on the saw, and slowly, almost tenderly, lowered the blade.

This James Newcastle fellow (assuming she'd guessed right) was quite handsome, she realized. With that thought came a jab of irritation — at herself. Why did she always immediately have to notice certain features in a man? Like this man's head of thick brown hair and neatly trimmed beard? Like the fact that he was tall, probably several inches taller than her, with broad shoulders and a trim waist and —

Urgh! Stop it! she ordered herself.

The man grabbed the piece of wood, took off his safety glasses, and examined the cut closely. He gently blew away a bit of sawdust and, after a pause, nodded to himself, as if satisfied.

Then something — had she made a noise? — broke his concentration. He turned her way and blinked with surprise.

"Hi," he said, his voice clear, his tone curious.

"Hi," she replied, frozen in place.

He set down the piece of wood, slipped off his safety glasses and ear muffs, and stepped toward her, hand outstretched. "Sorry, didn't hear you come in. You're Ms. Connelly, right? I'm James Newcastle."

The face beneath the beard was handsome, with friendly grey eyes and a wide mouth. There were flecks of grey in his beard, which suggested he was somewhere around forty. She'd been right about his height, too. And those shoulders of his really were quite broad and —

Urgh!

"Hello," she said, remembering at the last minute to extend her hand.

A jolt shot through her as their hands touched. His grip was warm and strong. She forced herself to stifle a gasp. Really, what in the world was wrong with her?

James, for his part, also seemed slightly taken aback, his eyes widening, as if surprised by something. After a brief pause, he said, "Pleased to meet you, Ms. Connelly."

"The pleasure is mine," she said, willing herself to sound calm and friendly. "And please, no Ms. Connelly. Melody is just fine."

Fortunately, the words managed to leave her mouth in a normal fashion. She felt herself beginning to settle down.

"Sorry about the noise down here," he said.

"Oh, no worries." Taking his cue, she shifted her attention to the transformation that had taken place. Gone forever was the dim, decrepit, dingy basement of a year ago. What greeted her now was a crisp new canvas for her future media room. The original brick-and-mortar foundation walls were now hidden behind insulated, moisture-proofed drywall. The original dirt floor was covered with polished concrete. New lighting in the new ceiling cast a warm, cheerful glow through the space. Along the far wall, a cluster of wires and cables protruded from a large socket, ready to be hooked up to a future big-screen TV.

When the space was finished, the media room would include theater seating, a huge TV, and a state-of-the-art sound system. Right now, it was still very much a work space. Canvas tarps covered the concrete floor to protect against scrapes and dings. The work table in the center of the room seemed to be all about woodworking, with a variety of tools and machines whose purposes she could only guess at.

"I can't believe how good everything looks," she said. "What a change."

"Luke and the crew did a great job."

"It used to be so scary. A horrid old basement — dark and damp and dank."

"Luke was telling me." He gestured to a corner. "A lot of work went into the foundation, especially over there, to address leaks and rot."

"Don't I know it," she sighed, remembering the phone calls and emails.

"The good news is, it's all tight and water-proofed now." His gaze swung upward. "They did a nice job with the lighting and wiring and sound system, too. This'll be a great place for movies and TV."

She gestured to the table. "Luke mentioned you're doing the woodwork?"

"Molding and trim and other finishing touches. It made sense to set up here on site. I hope that's okay."

"Oh, yes, of course." She pointed to the piece of wood he'd just cut. "What's that piece for?"

"This little guy," he said, picking it up and handing it to her, "will replace a section of window trim in the attic. An old window up there had leaked for years, and part of the trim had warped."

The piece of wood felt so light and small, almost inconsequential, yet the care with which James had cut it suggested it had a very specific and necessary purpose.

She handed it back with a smile. Now that they had a topic to talk about — the house — she found herself relaxing, her natural curiosity asserting itself. "How does that work? When you find a piece of wood that's damaged, do you have to replace the whole piece?"

"I try to reuse as much of the original wood as possible. This piece will replace a damaged section of trim. Once it's in place and sanded and painted, it'll look like it's always been there."

Her eyes landed on something she hadn't noticed before. On the floor next to the work table was an animal crate.

And peering up at her from inside were the curious eyes of a cat!

"Who do we have here?" she said, stepping closer for a better look.

"That's Buster. He's not too happy with me right now."

As she got closer, she saw why. The cat was wearing a white cone collar around his neck and a bandage on his right front leg. "What happened to the poor fellow?"

"He got into a fight," James said with a sigh. "Probably a raccoon, we're not sure. The vet patched him up and he's going to be fine — a full recovery. But until the stitches come off, he's stuck with that collar."

Buster gave Melody a plaintive *meow*. Melody smiled. "How much longer?"

"Two more days."

"Poor fellow."

"Poor annoyed fellow."

"And you brought him with you because…."

"It didn't feel right to leave him home alone." James gave her a wry grin. "Plus, he has a knack for trouble. I wanted to keep an eye on him."

"Oh, is that so?" She leaned closer. "Are you a troublemaker, Buster?"

Buster responded with another plaintive *meow*.

"He likes being in charge. King of the castle. When his world suits him, he's about as friendly as they come. But when he's bothered by something, watch out."

Melody chuckled. "He sounds delightful."

"Most of the time."

A thought came. "The poor darling needs a distraction. Something to take his mind off his woes."

"What are you suggesting?"

"You're free to let him out, if you're comfortable doing that."

James's eyebrows rose. "He'll want to explore."

"Oh, that's fine."

"He'll want to inspect every nook and cranny."

"The house has a lot of those."

"Before you know it, he'll decide he owns the place."

"Oh, no worries."

"There'll be no stopping him. When I say he's the boss, I'm not joking."

Melody laughed. "He's welcome to everything here."

He reached down, his hand on the door latch, his grey eyes looking up at her for confirmation. "Last chance."

"Let him out, darling. Set him free!"

"Just remember, this was your idea." He opened the door and stepped back.

A few seconds later, Buster's head emerged. He stood still, surveying his surroundings, then strode forward. He was a large cat, sleek and powerful, with thick grey fur. Even with the bandage on his paw and the plastic cone around his neck, he held himself proudly.

"How old is he?" Melody asked.

"About two, we think."

"You think?"

"We found him at our back door last year. My daughter started feeding him, and before we knew it, he'd moved in."

"So he's an indoor-outdoor cat?"

"He's an everything cat."

Melody bent down and stuck out her hand. Buster regarded her silently, then moved closer and sniffed. He gave her another *meow* and stared up at her some more, like he was making up his mind.

Then he moved closer and rubbed himself against her boot, his fur sliding over the leather.

"He likes you," James said.

Melody reached down to pet him. His fur was thick and wonderfully soft.

He purred at her touch and rubbed himself some more. Once again, he turned his gaze upward as if to say: *Nice lady, will you please help me out of this darn collar? Purrrty purrrrty please?*

"I can guess what he wants," Melody said.

"He has a knack for making his wishes clear."

Buster glanced toward James, as if warning him that he understood every word and didn't appreciate the play-by-play commentary.

Returning his attention to Melody, he *meowed* again.

"Sorry, Buster," Melody said softly. "That collar is for your own good. Just another day or two."

Buster's eyes narrowed. *No more petting for you, pretty lady,* he seemed to say. With a flick of his tail, he turned and began a thorough investigation of his new surroundings. There was no hesitation in his movements, every step and sniff sure.

When his gaze landed on the stairs, he dashed right up.

"And he's off," Melody said.

"And he's off," James said.

She returned her attention to James and found a smile on his face. There was interest in his gaze, she saw, along with something else: appreciation.

"You're good with him," he said, referring to Buster.

"How's that?"

"You're friendly, but no pushover."

"Ah."

"He respects that."

"Oh, he does, does he?"

"I know where he's coming from."

"Oh, you do, do you?"

He flushed, as if realizing he'd perhaps said too much. "I mean, I like how you've been making renovation decisions."

"What do you mean?" she said, her brow furrowing.

"I've been onsite the past couple of weeks, so I've noticed how you and Luke work together."

"Ah," she said, curious. "Tell me more."

"You don't hesitate. You don't second-guess yourself. You and Luke talk through options, you decide what you want, and Luke gets moving on it. A lot of homeowners have trouble making decisions. They agonize over every little thing, which causes delays and cost increases and more."

Melody shrugged. "I probably would have dilly-dallied more if I had the option. But the show I was in took up nearly all of my time. Luke and I had only a few minutes each day to catch up."

"You put those minutes to good use. I'm amazed at how quickly he and his crew powered through the work here."

At that moment, they heard Clara upstairs calling Melody's name.

"Clara, down here!" Melody yelled, using her stage voice to project.

Clara made her way downstairs and blinked when she saw James.

"Hey, Mr. Newcastle," she said.

"Clara," he said, "you've got to start calling me James. You aren't a kid anymore."

Clara looked at him sheepishly. "You're absolutely right, *James*. See? I did it." She turned to Melody and explained, "I used to babysit for *James*'s daughter back in high school."

"You mean Anna," Melody said.

Two pairs of eyes swung toward her, surprised.

"I met her last night at the bookstore," Melody continued, in answer to their unspoken question. "She seems like a wonderful young woman."

James nodded and grinned, clearly pleased.

"Anna's great," Clara said. "Hate to change the

subject, but did you know there's a cat upstairs? Wearing a cone collar?"

"Big and grey? Acting like he's in charge?" James said.

Clara laughed. "Exactly."

"That's Buster."

Melody added, "The poor thing needed a distraction, something to take his mind off his troubles, so we decided to let him explore."

Clara's gaze landed on the animal crate and comprehension dawned. "Got it." She turned to Melody. "Listen, hate to have to ask, but something's come up and I have to get back to town. Would it be okay if…?"

"If I drive you?" Melody said. "Of course." She turned to James. "I'll be back this afternoon. Lots of shopping to do. Lots of moving in to start."

"I'm planning to be here most of the day, if that's all right with you."

"Yes, of course."

"Then I'll see you later." The way he said it, the words sounded like a promise.

She felt a flutter in her chest as she realized she rather liked the idea of him being here when she returned. "See you soon."

$\mathcal{M}$ elody and Clara hopped into the SUV and got moving, slipping past the trees along the winding gravel drive to Summit Lane.

"So what's the problem down there?" Melody asked.

Clara stared at her phone, which had just buzzed again, her brow creased with frustration. "The mayor tracked down the electric saw we use for road clearing, but something's wrong with the battery. It isn't holding its charge."

"Meaning?"

"We can hook the saw up to the truck and power it that way, but doing that takes longer because we have to position the truck closer to the fallen tree or branch or whatever's blocking the road, and then we have to run a cord, and then we have to get everything wrapped back up."

"And that means?"

"Most of the time, a cord is fine. If a tree falls across a road, getting the truck close enough to run a cord is easy. But if the tree falls in such a way that we need to go into the woods to make the cuts — up or down a ridge, for example — relying on a cord for power is trickier."

"Sounds like there could be a safety issue."

She nodded. "Depending on the situation. Bottom line: If the battery isn't working, it'll take longer to clear the roads when the storm hits."

"When, not if?"

Clara nodded. "According to the latest forecast, we're looking at ice, not snow."

Melody swallowed back her uneasiness. "What's the timing?"

"Starting this afternoon."

Melody glanced up at the sky, which was still clear and blue. "The idea of a storm on a day like this...."

"Hey, no need to worry. Whatever happens, we'll be fine."

"So what are Plans B, C, and D? I know you have them."

Clara threw Melody a quick smile. "Luke has saws we can use, but they're smaller than what he and the mayor say we really need if a big tree comes down."

"So your job is to...?"

"My job is to hunt down a backup battery for the big saw."

Melody shook her head. "Life in a small town is full of surprises."

Clara shrugged. "Never-ending."

"What's your plan of attack?"

"First stop is the salvage yard. There might be a battery there. Jim — he's the owner — doesn't have a mobile phone and he isn't at his desk. He's probably out in his warehouse."

"So you need to swing by in person."

"Right."

"And if he doesn't have one?"

Clara gave her a tight smile. "Then I start making calls. Lots of folks have electric saws, but I'm not sure they have the kind we need."

Clara's phone buzzed again and she read the incoming text. As she started typing a response, Melody found her attention wandering to the unexpected encounter she'd just had in her new media room.

That fellow, James Newcastle — she had a good feeling about him. He was handsome, of course, but what really struck her was his attention to detail. Clearly, the quality of his work mattered to him. The attention he'd given that tiny piece of trim was revealing. Her gut told her he applied the same level of care to other parts of his life.

Like his cat Buster, the stray who'd shown up at

his back door and lucked into a good home. And his daughter Anna at the bookstore, who seemed like a confident young woman, friendly and cheerful and hardworking.

But there was no point in thinking about James right now, she reminded herself. Certainly not today, with a storm approaching and a mountain of tasks on her plate.

Clara was still typing away, so Melody took a moment to engage in a habit she'd picked up from an actor friend years earlier — a habit that involved asking herself two important questions:

At this moment in my life, what matters most?

What do I want to commit myself to, fully and without reservation?

The answers came, as they often did, as simple declarative statements from the universe:

She wanted to turn her newly renovated house into her new second home.

She wanted to discover the next chapter in her life.

And — most immediately — she wanted to create a wonderful Christmas for her mom and Benny.

Because *this* was the year she would finally do Christmas right.

Without warning, she found herself thinking again about James's handsome face and lively grey eyes. Which she found puzzling, even as she acknowledged the flutter of attraction. Clearly, on some level, the possibility of romance — if not with James, then with someone? — held a certain appeal. Perhaps romance deserved a place on her wish list as well?

Not right now, she told herself. *Maybe after the holiday. Maybe after you have a house you can live in and a kitchen you can cook in. Maybe after you and your mom have the best Christmas you've ever had.*

The road leveled out as they reached the valley floor and headed toward town.

Clara set her phone down and sighed.

Melody glanced over. "Penny for your thoughts, darling."

"Sorry, just a lot to sort through," Clara said.

"There's no one better at sorting and organizing than you. Where am I taking you?"

"The hardware store, if that's okay."

"Of course. I have shopping to do there anyway."

Clara smiled. "Sorry I can't tag along with you today."

"We need to figure out how to clone you."

"I know, right? One of me could deal with the electric saw...."

"While another you relaxes in a bubble bath."

Clara laughed as the town square appeared ahead.

"So how are your dad and Peggy? How's married life treating them?"

Clara nodded. "They're good. The wedding was

beautiful." She paused, as if collecting her thoughts. "Peggy's moved into our — dad's — house."

Melody waited for Clara to say more. It had been twelve years since Clara lost her mom to breast cancer. And as much as Clara liked and appreciated Peggy, and as happy as Clara was that her dad had found a new person to share his life with, the change hadn't been without emotional difficulties.

"So … everything working out?" Melody said, after it became clear that Clara wasn't going to say more without prompting.

"Oh, fine. It's just…."

After another pause, Melody said gently, "It's just what?"

"I'm really happy for Dad and I really like Peggy," Clara said. "It's just that…."

"It's hard to see changes in the house you grew up in. The house you lived in with your mom."

Clara nodded. "Exactly. I mean, I know changes can be good, but…."

"They can also be challenging."

Clara shook herself, as if clearing her thoughts. "This change is both. Good for Dad and Peggy, a bit challenging for me. But that's okay. They're happy, and that's what matters most. At the end of the day, that's what makes me happiest, too."

"You're a good daughter. You know that, right?"

Clara gave her a grateful smile. For just a second,

the years melted away and Melody caught a glimpse of the young girl her friend had once been.

Melody slipped into a parking spot across the street from Cane Hardware and shut off the engine. "We're here. Everything good?"

"Everything's good. All systems go."

They stepped out of the SUV and made their way across the street.

"By the way," Melody said, recalling her walk past the hardware store the previous night, "congratulations on the window display. Stunning work."

"Thanks," Clara said, beaming. "It was a joint effort, me and Peggy."

They made their way into the store, which was packed with holiday shoppers. Behind the register, Melody's eyes landed on Clara's new stepmom. Peggy was in her mid-forties, with a warm, open face and shoulder-length brown hair pulled back into a ponytail. She was dressed in jeans and a red Cane Hardware sweatshirt. She glanced up as they entered, then did a double-take of recognition.

"Melody!" Peggy said, then slipped around the counter to give her a quick hug. "Welcome back."

"Peggy, so good to see you."

"I heard you got in last night."

"Just in time for an evening stroll past your gorgeous window display. You've outdone yourselves this year. Congratulations."

"Thank you. It was a real team effort." Peggy turned to Clara. "Hey, you. Your dad's checking out back for a battery."

"Thanks, Peggy."

Peggy gestured to the register. "I should get back to…."

"Of course," Melody said. "I'll be loading up on supplies. See you in a bit!"

With Clara in the lead, they wound their way through the store, easing past customers crowding the aisles, and headed toward the storage area in the back, where they found Ted, Clara's dad and the owner of the store, typing away into a computer. He was a big, rough-and-tumble guy, dressed in blue coveralls and a blue Cane Hardware sweatshirt, a tool belt wrapped around his waist, his bald pate gleaming under the overhead light. A grin lit up his face when he recognized who Clara had with her.

"Melody," he said, standing up to give her a quick hug. "Merry Christmas!"

"Merry Christmas, Ted. So good to see you."

In the two years since Melody had first met him, so much had changed. Two years ago, Ted and Peggy had just started dating — and now they were married. Two years ago, Clara had been single — and now she was married.

Two years ago, Melody had been freshly dumped by her movie-star boyfriend and, desperate to escape the pain of the breakup, had impulsively decided to travel to her P.R. assistant's hometown right before Christmas.

And now? Two years later, she was a homeowner, her former P.R. assistant was her good friend, her mom was on her way to spend Christmas with her, and, while she was still very much single, she was —

What, exactly? She sent the question out into the universe. It was an important question to ask, she sensed. Beyond a few first dates, she hadn't really dated since Derek.

How did she feel about that?

She was okay with her current single status, she decided.

Sort of.

At least for now.

Unless…?

She became aware again of her surroundings and Ted beaming at her.

"Ted, you're looking great. Married life suits you."

"You're right about that. How are you?"

"Fine, just fine. And thrilled to be here. Word of warning: You'll be seeing a lot of me. I'm about to become your best customer."

He laughed. "That's a lot of house you just bought. Anything you need, any questions, let me know."

"So, Dad," Clara said, pointing to the computer. "Any luck?"

He shook his head. "We don't have a battery in stock. I've placed an order, but it'll take a week to get here."

"I was thinking of the salvage yard...."

He nodded. "Worth a shot."

"And if I strike out there?"

"I can help with calls."

"Car keys?"

"Usual place."

Clara turned to Melody. "I should probably be heading out...."

"Of course, darling. Thank you for coming out with me to explore this morning."

"Wouldn't have missed it for the world. See you in a bit?"

"See you soon!"

Clara said to her dad, "I'll text and let you know."

"Got it," he said.

They watched Clara head toward the back exit.

"I'm so glad she moved back home," he said.

"Heartsprings Valley is lucky to have her," Melody agreed.

Ted's eyes twinkled. "And lucky to have *you*. So, you're here to stock up."

Melody nodded. "My new home is completely bare, and I simply must do something about that."

"We have baskets and carts up front. Need anything, just holler."

"Oh, I will," Melody said, her excitement increasing as she contemplated the shopping extravaganza about to unfold. "I most certainly will!"

CHAPTER 13

*O*kay, so maybe *extravaganza* wasn't quite the right description for the plethora of purchases she was making, she thought as she pushed her shopping cart down the tight aisles, her eyes wandering over household items of all kinds. Perhaps *smorgasbord* was a better term? After all, her purchases were mostly household essentials, not extravagances — the everyday items that every home needed. And she needed so many different things!

She forced herself to move slowly and methodically, her hands reaching out to pluck items as they appeared before her. One of the disadvantages of living in New York was that she didn't have space to store a lot of extra stuff — stuff that could have come in handy now that she had a big house and more rooms than she'd ever dreamed possible. Did she need a broom? Yes. And a mop, and a duster, and a rake, and a vacuum cleaner, and extra vacuum bags, and towels and dish rags and —

With a start, she realized her cart was full. *Oh, dear.* Simple logistics dictated that she was going to have to do her shopping in stages, one cart at a time. She got into line and soon enough reached Peggy at the register.

"Round one," Melody said as Peggy rung up her purchases.

Peggy smiled. "Need help carrying anything?"

"I don't think so. I'm parked across the street. Can I take the cart out with me?"

"Of course. See you in a bit."

And so it went. Four shopping carts full of household necessities and four trips out to her SUV, the back of which started looking rather full. She'd become familiar with the hardware store two years earlier, when she and Clara had spent an afternoon here, working on the Christmas window display. But now, with her shopping expedition taking her up and down every inch of every aisle, she was quickly becoming an expert.

She'd finished her fourth round and was cramming paper towels and toilet paper into the back of the SUV when a gust of wind hit her. A blustery gust, wet with foreboding. She looked upward. The blue sky was gone, replaced by grey overcast.

Anxiously, she took out her phone and typed a

message to her mom: "Checking in. How's the drive treating you?"

She had enough basic items for now, she decided. Best to get her bounty up to the house. Without doubt she'd forgotten stuff, but she could sort that out later. She brought the empty cart back into the store.

"I'm heading out," she told Peggy. "See you soon."

"See you soon," Peggy said with a smile. "Merry Christmas!"

As Melody hopped into her SUV, her phone vibrated. Her mom had texted back: "Drive is lovely. See you around 5!"

Melody sighed, relieved but anxious nonetheless. Clara was right, of course: There was no point worrying about things that were out of her control. But how exactly did one avoid doing that? When bad weather hit New York, she could stay inside and order takeout. But up here, people were forced to interact with the elements. How did one stop oneself from worrying about the power and fury of Mother Nature?

Cut it out, she ordered herself. She'd drive herself insane if she didn't stay focused on what she had to do. Clara was right. She should listen to her friend. Clara was a local who knew the score, who understood how the weather worked up here, and who knew how to respond to whatever nature threw at them.

With a sigh, she turned on the engine and pulled out. The roads were becoming familiar to her now. Soon enough she'd be driving them with the confidence of a native.

As she climbed the ridge road, she glanced through a gap in the trees toward the east, toward the line of low mountains across the lake. Clara had said the storm would come from that direction. Aside from the grey overcast sky, she saw no indication yet of what would soon arrive.

She passed a house and, through the front windows, saw the lights of a Christmas tree, and realized —

Christmas decorations! She resisted the urge to smack her forehead. She'd been so focused on cleaning supplies and coffee filters and garbage bags that she'd completely blanked on all of the lovely ornaments and wreaths and garlands and lights and so much more that her new home so desperately needed. The hardware store had a nice selection, too — already she was envisioning some of them in her new home, adding holiday cheer.

Clara wouldn't have forgotten about an entire category of purchases, she thought somewhat gloomily. Her friend would have walked into the hardware store *prepared*. Today was one of those days when an actual list — written down on actual paper — would have come in handy.

But there was nothing she could do about that now. Turning onto the ridge road, she headed up toward Summit Lane. The grey skies above were hiding the sun. Already, the day was half over. When she got to the house, she'd unload as quickly as she could and head back down for more shopping. She needed groceries for her empty refrigerator and —

A Christmas tree! At the thought of getting one, her spirits lifted. Yes, there had to be a Christmas tree lot or farm nearby. She'd text Clara for directions.

Good humor restored, she reached Summit Lane and, when she reached the top, turned onto her newly refinished gravel drive. The trees really were quite lovely, she thought again. Tall and old, with thick branches that captured the light, they'd been growing for decades. With clouds overhead, the path through them was dim enough that, for a few seconds, Melody considered turning on her headlights.

But then, as if the universe was telling her not to bother, she reached the open meadow and the afternoon light returned. Her new home came into view, beckoning her forward. She parked as close as she could to the side door leading up to the kitchen.

For the first time, she noticed a dark blue SUV parked at the rear of the house — James's, most likely. After hopping out and grabbing as many items as she could, she carried them awkwardly to the side door and, after fumbling for her house key, managed to open the door and step inside. She dumped everything on the kitchen counter, then went back outside for the next round.

When she returned to the kitchen, arms overloaded with supplies, she found James there. "Heard you come in," he said. "Here, let me help with that."

"Thank you," she said gratefully.

Quickly, he took items from her arms and set them on the counter. "Any more outside?"

"Oh, yes."

"I'll help."

Before she could say no, he was out the door. She followed him to the SUV and watched him load up with most of the rest of her purchases.

"You don't have to do this," she said, not meaning it.

"Happy to help."

She smiled, glad to hear him say that. Gathering up the last few items from the SUV, she followed him inside.

"How's the woodworking coming?" she asked as she set her purchases on the counter.

"Making progress, one piece of trim at a time." He gestured toward the supplies. "Where do you want these to go?"

"That's a very good question," she said, her eyes roving over her seemingly endless cabinets. She felt a jolt of anticipation — she had so many options! "I have no idea. And I get to figure that out!"

He grinned as he picked up on her excitement. "I'm guessing it's a different story back in New York?"

"Night and day, darling. Storage in New York is a precision affair, every inch of space accounted for."

At that moment, as if nature was reminding her of its presence, a gust of wind rattled the windows.

He followed her glance and frowned. "We'll see ice and snow later."

She sighed. "I should probably head back out and get more stuff before the storm hits."

He gestured toward the counter. "You're off to a pretty good start."

"Pretty good," she agreed. "But there's so much more. I completely forgot about Christmas decorations, and those are a must!"

"The hardware store has a good selection."

"Oh, definitely." A thought came. "Is there a Christmas tree lot or farm I can visit?"

"Sure. Abner's Tree Farm is the place to go. It's along the main valley road as you head toward town. Look for the sign on the right. You can't miss it."

"Thank you."

"I take it you're planning to get a tree right now?"

"Christmas wouldn't be Christmas without it."

He paused, as if he wanted to say something, then

ran his gaze over the items on the counter. "You'll need a tree stand and a liner."

"Consider them added to the list."

"Abner should have them."

"Sounds good."

His brow furrowed, almost as if he was concerned about her plan to get a tree right now by herself. Really, it was rather adorable.

"Darling, I'll be fine," she said, eager to reassure him. "I'm stronger than I look."

"Oh, it's not that," James said, looking momentarily abashed. "It's just that...." He paused, then said, "Do you have rope?"

Melody blinked as she realized: *Nope to the rope.* She'd seen some at the hardware store, but hadn't even thought to get it.

"Abner will have some," James said. "Have him tie the tree to the top for you."

His concern was touching, actually. A thought came — maybe she could ask him to come with her. But she immediately rejected the idea. They were strangers, after all. Plus, he was here to fix up her house, not help with errands.

"I promise you," she said firmly, "I'll be fine."

Another gust hit the windows.

"Clearly, the universe is telling me to get moving," she said.

He reached into his pocket and pulled out his card. "My phone number. Call if you need anything."

"Thanks."

He stood there for a second, clearly torn by inde-cision, then said, "Listen. How about I come with you for the tree?"

"Oh, there's no need," she said reflexively. "I'll be fine."

"I'll feel better knowing you have someone to help. You're new here and there's no telling when the storm will hit and...."

He really did look adorable, she realized. There was something so appealing about his concern.

"Are you sure?" she heard herself say.

"Of course," he said, a relieved smile appearing. "It's not that I think you can't do it yourself. It's just that...."

"Well, then thank you," she said, unsure if she should be kicking herself for giving in to her concerns, or giving herself a round of applause for recruiting help. "I guess we should head out."

"After you," he said with a smile, gesturing toward the door.

CHAPTER 14

*I*t really was very sweet of him to volunteer, she told herself again as the two of them wound their way in her SUV down the long gravel driveway toward Summit Lane. He hadn't needed to, and she probably didn't really need him to be there with her, but the truth was — she found his company reassuring. There was a solidity to this James fellow, an aura of capability that she appreciated.

On the other side of the windshield, daylight was beginning to fade, the thick grey clouds overhead getting thicker. She flipped on her headlights and focused on the path ahead.

"Thank you again for offering to help," she said.

"Not a problem."

"I can't believe how quickly the day has gone by, and there's still so much to do."

"What's on your list?"

"The tree, of course," she said as turned onto Summit Lane and headed down. "But also, if there's time, groceries and Christmas ornaments at the hardware store before heading back to the Inn — that's where I'm staying — to make sure everything's ready for my mom and her husband."

"You mom's coming up here for Christmas?"

"She and Benny — her husband — get in around five."

He glanced east and she followed suit, blinking when she realized what she wasn't seeing. The mountains on the other side of the lake — clearly visible earlier — had vanished in a cloud of grey.

A chill ran through her, despite the car heater pumping out lots of lovely warmth. Mother Nature sure didn't play around, and the visual evidence was sobering.

She sensed what James was thinking:

The sooner her mom arrived, the better.

"Do you like Christmas songs?" she asked.

"I love 'em."

She turned on the radio and smiled as an old favorite about chestnuts roasting filled the car.

"Tell me about Broadway," he said suddenly, without warning.

"Broadway?" she repeated, startled.

"Sorry," he said with an apologetic smile. "That was a bit abrupt, wasn't it? My daughter Anna is a big Broadway fan. She'll never forgive me if I don't ask."

Melody chuckled. "Your daughter mentioned that. She seems like a wonderful young woman."

"You said you met her last night at the bookstore?"

"That's right. She talked about you."

"Really?" he said, surprised.

"She said her dad was the artist who made my new dining table."

"Ah."

Something in his tone made her look over. He seemed hesitant, perhaps even embarrassed. Which she found surprising. He hadn't struck her as shy, but perhaps he was?

"I haven't seen the actual table yet," she said. "My house tour hasn't taken me as far as the dining room."

"Well, I hope you like it."

"Oh, I already know I do," she hastened to assure him. "Luke sent me photos. It looks gorgeous. I can't wait to see it in person."

She reached the valley road and turned right. Almost immediately, she saw a sign: "Abner's Tree Farm — 1 mile."

"So," she said, "you asked about Broadway."

"Sorry. A vague question about a big topic."

"Oh, that's fine. It's a good question, actually — it gets me thinking. I like asking myself big questions every now and then."

"All right, then. Tell me about Broadway."

"Broadway is...." She paused, waiting for the words to come. "For the last five years, Broadway has been home."

"Home," he repeated.

"In the past five years, I've spent more time in rehearsal rooms and theaters than anywhere else. Broadway is where my friends and colleagues, the people who have become my extended family, are."

"Sounds like home to me."

"It's also where my dreams have come true."

"Tell me more."

This James fellow was a good listener, she realized. He was easy to talk with. There was a sense of assurance with him. Perhaps that was simply because she was in a car with him, the sounds of Christmas playing in the background. But her gut was telling her otherwise.

I'm feeling comfortable because he's someone I can feel comfortable with.

She took a deep breath. "I was twenty when I moved to New York. Like every other acting-singing-dancing wannabe who moves to New York, I had a burning ambition to perform. I wanted to sing and dance my way to stardom. And for years and years and years, that was my focus — my only focus. Everything I did was about achieving my dream. For years, I studied my craft and worked long hours as a waitress and went on countless auditions and got rejected and rejected and rejected until...."

She paused, surprised to hear the flood of words coming out of her mouth. "Sorry, I got off track. That's probably not what you want to hear about."

"No, I do," he said, then pointed to the sign for Abner's Tree Farm up ahead. "The next right is where you turn."

With a nod, she turned off the main road onto a winding country lane. Up ahead, the road began to rise. A hill came into view, decorated with row upon row of Christmas trees. At the foot of the hill were a farmhouse and a barn. She pulled into the parking area in front just as another car was heading out, a big tree strapped to its roof. Inside the car, she caught a glimpse of a mom and dad in the front seat and two smiling kids in back.

She glanced over at James and found him looking at her. "So, what kind of tree do you want?" he said.

"Big and bushy and beautiful," she said immediately.

He grinned. "There are a couple of different varieties...."

"Which I know nothing about."

"So ... I guess you'll know it when we see it."

"Exactly," she said, pleased.

After hopping out of the SUV, they made their way to the barn, where a thin, older man in heavy winter gear was placing a tree into what looked like a metal box planter. They were the only ones here, she realized as she looked around. Fascinated, Melody watched as the metal box shook the tree vigorously, sending a few loose needles flying. The man took the tree, turned it on its side, and stuck the base of it into a machine that looked like a jet engine on a cart. He turned the machine on and fed the tree into the jet engine. When the tree emerged on the other side, it was wrapped in twine.

"I've never seen that done," she said.

The man looked up from his work and squinted at them. "That you, James? I'm getting ready to close up for the day."

"Good to see you, Abner," James said. "Hope there's time for one more customer."

Abner leaned the wrapped-up tree against the barn door and turned his attention to Melody, squinting some more.

"Don't know you, do I?" Abner said to her.

"Melody," she said, stepping forward to shake his hand. He had a wizened face — in his seventies, if she had to guess — and moved with ease, probably because his work kept him active.

"She's after a big, bushy, beautiful tree," James said.

"We got a few of those. Top of the slope." He pointed up. "Best you hurry."

"What's your sense?" James said.

"Any minute now. Wet, too."

James shook his head. "Saw?"

Abner reached behind him, grabbed a hand saw from a nearby bench, and handed it over, then pointed at a big cart with sturdy wheels. "Take that, too."

"Back in a bit," James said, then turned to Melody and handed her the saw. "You take this and I'll get the cart."

"Got it."

James took hold of the cart and started toward the hill. "This way."

"Nice meeting you, Abner," Melody said.

"Pleasure's mine, young lady," Abner replied.

She followed James up the slope, hurrying to keep up. Usually she was the one who walked fast, but his long legs were clearly capable of speed as well, even with the cart in tow.

"So the wet reference back there?" she asked. "Is that about the storm?"

"Abner's a walking, talking weather forecast. Never known him to be wrong."

The air was cold up here, but not excessively so. "But wet? What does that mean?"

"It means the storm will fall as freezing rain and turn into ice when it hits the ground."

"And since ice is heavier than snow," she added, remembering what Luke had said, "the extra weight means more branches and power lines coming down."

"Right. And icy roads."

Suddenly the darkening sky seemed more ominous. A thought came: Perhaps the tree could wait. But almost immediately, she pushed back with: They were already here, trudging up a hill, past lines of lovely evergreens, one of which would make a wonderful Christmas tree for her new house — a tree that she and her mom would decorate together as part of her perfect Christmas dream.

As they neared the top of the hill, she saw it: A large, beautifully shaped tree.

Waiting for her.

"There," she said, pointing. "That's the one."

"I like how you decide. No hesitation."

"When you know, you know."

"She's a beauty all right." He pointed to the saw in her hand. "You want to do the honors?"

She shook her head. "Um…."

He grinned. "No worries." He reached for the saw, then turned toward the tree, knelt down, and started sawing. Within seconds, she heard a sharp crack.

He stood up. "Stand back."

She retreated a few steps.

"Here she comes," he said.

Reaching through the thick branches, he gave the tree a push and –

Down it came!

"Okay," he said. "If you could make sure the cart stays put...."

She stepped forward and gripped the handle. James grabbed the base of the tree and wrestled it onto the cart. It was a big tree, and no doubt heavy, but he moved it with ease.

Branches brushed her face and she breathed in the fresh evergreen scent. Yes, the tree was perfect. Already she could see it in her new home, festooned with all manner of lights and ornaments.

"Can I confess how glad I am that you volunteered to help me?" she said a moment later as she followed him down the hill.

He smiled. "A bit of a workout, but that's good — gets the heart pumping."

When they reached the barn, James knew exactly what to do. With Abner's help, he stuck the tree into the box that shook the branches free of loose needles and then into the second machine that wrapped it tightly in twine.

"What else you need?" Abner asked.

"The works," James said.

Abner grunted and went into the barn.

"What's he getting?" Melody asked.

"He sells a complete kit — stand, pan, liner, and rope."

Melody smiled, impressed. "Quite an operation."

"He's been doing it for decades. As long as I can remember."

Abner returned with a cardboard box, which he handed to James.

Melody reached into her winter coat for her wallet. "How much do I owe you?"

Abner pointed overhead. "Wife already took the cash box and card doohickey into the house. Best you hurry along. You can come by and settle up after the storm."

"Are you sure?"

"Yes, time to go. You two be safe out there."

"Thank you, Abner. Merry Christmas!"

"Merry Christmas to you."

CHAPTER 15

"Wow," Melody said as they pulled out a moment later, "Abner seemed anxious for us to go."

"He just wants us safe at home as soon as possible."

"Works for me. What Abner wants, Abner gets. Let's head back to the house so you can get your SUV and we'll both call it a day."

"Sounds good."

As they reached the main road and turned left, she heard and saw the first *splat-splat-splat* of freezing rain hitting the windshield. "As promised, the storm is here," she said with a sigh.

James glanced at her dashboard. "You're almost out of gas."

"What?" A quick glance confirmed he was right.

"There's a gas station just past the turnoff to the ridge road. Better to fill up while you can."

She nodded, her sense of foreboding increasing. Everyone, it seemed, was taking the storm seriously. All day, no matter who she'd been with, the storm had been on their minds.

They drove past the turnoff to the ridge road and Melody spied the gas station up ahead. It was an older place — a ramshackle building fronted by two ancient gas pumps beneath a tall awning, like an old-time photograph come to life.

She pulled in next to a pump.

"I'll fill up," James said.

"And I'll go inside and pay. You need anything?"

He shook his head. "I'm good."

She made her way inside, a bell tinkling her arrival. The interior felt like a throwback, too — hearkening back to the days when gas stations were mostly owned and operated by locals. Wooden shelves lined the walls. The floor was worn linoleum, probably decades old. In the back, an antique fridge with a glass door held a small selection of cold sodas.

At the register, a middle-aged woman looked up from her knitting. "Hello, dear."

"Here to fill up," Melody said as her gaze landed on the selection of candies and snacks on the shelves.

You never know, she thought. *Just in case.* "Maybe some snacks as well," she said.

The woman nodded. "Especially with a storm like this one."

"What's the latest?"

"They're saying half an inch of freezing rain in the next couple of hours."

"That sounds like a lot."

The woman nodded. "You'll be fine, as long as you get back home soon."

Quickly, Melody started grabbing items at random and stacking them at the cash register.

The woman set down her knitting and rang the items up, then got everything into a bag.

"Drive safely, young lady," the woman said as she handed over the bag.

"Thank you," Melody replied, then stepped outside.

James had finished filling the tank and was putting the gas nozzle back on the pump.

"Ready?" he said, then gestured to the bag. "Here, let me."

"Thank you." She handed him the bag, then climbed into the SUV. James joined her, bag on his lap, and they headed off.

The precipitation was falling steadily now, wet and almost slushy, her windshield wipers doing their best to keep the view ahead clear. She turned onto the ridge road, maintaining a steady pace.

Next to her, James peeked inside the bag. "Preparing for a siege?"

She laughed. "I don't know, I guess I just figured, the way everyone has been acting today...."

He shrugged. "Better safe than sorry."

"Right."

Daylight was almost gone now. Melody kept her eyes glued to the road, driving steadily, taking the ridge road's switchback turns carefully.

"The woman in the gas station said we're getting half an inch of rain in the next two hours."

James whistled softly. "That's a lot."

"If it all freezes, that means a lot of ice, right?"

"That's right."

He wasn't sugarcoating his concern, she realized. She reached Summit Lane and turned. They'd be back at the house soon. They would unload the tree, James would get into his SUV, and they'd both head back down to town, where soon enough they'd both be safe and sound inside.

Without warning, the SUV slipped on the road. The slide lasted just a second — they regained traction almost instantly — but Melody couldn't restrain her gasp, her fingers tightening on the steering wheel.

"We're fine," James said. "Nothing to worry about. Almost there."

Melody exhaled with relief when she saw the mailbox for her house. *They'd made it.* "Thank goodness," she said as she turned onto her gravel driveway.

She glanced over at James and realized he wasn't sharing her sense of relief, at least not yet. He seemed tense, his eyes gazing upward.

With a jolt, she realized why: The lovely old trees they were driving through had big branches — branches that were getting coated with ice and heavier by the second.

It was only when they cleared the woods and reached the open meadow that she sensed him relax.

She parked in front of the house and he said, "Let's get the tree onto the covered front porch. It got wet on the drive up, so you'll want to get the ice off before you bring it inside."

"Got it," she said. They hopped out of the car. Freezing rain began soaking her coat and plastering her hair and face as she ran around the car to his side. Quickly, James untied the tree from the roof, slid it off the SUV, and reached down to grab the base of the tree with both arms. She wrapped her arms around the top.

"Ready," she said.

"Step carefully."

Together, they made their way to the house and up the steps, then lay the tree on the covered porch.

"It'll be good here for now," he said. "If it warms up tomorrow, most of the ice will melt away."

She shook her coat, brushing off water, then ran her gloved hand over her wet hair. Teeth chattering, she found her house key and managed to get it into the lock and push open the door.

James followed her in, then pushed the door shut behind him. His hand found the light switch.

As the old chandelier above her head filled the entry hall with a warm glow, Melody felt herself calming down.

James was frowning at the floor, now covered with water dripping from both of them. "Um," he said, "I don't remember doormats from your hardware store haul."

"That's because I didn't buy any," she said. "One of many things I forgot."

"But I did see towels…."

"Good idea."

Together, they headed into the kitchen. Melody grabbed two big fluffy towels and handed one to James. She ran her towel over her head and shoulders, then dropped the towel to the ground and pushed it over their wet steps through the kitchen entry back to the front door.

James, following behind her, did the same with his towel, then he folded his towel in half and set it in front of the door.

"Temporary doormat," he said.

"Thank you," she said. "And thank you again for helping with the tree. There's no way I could have managed that on my own."

"We should get a move on. I've got a cat to find."

Her eyes widened — she'd forgotten about poor Buster! "I hope he was okay being here alone."

"Oh, he's fine. Probably still exploring. I have some cat food downstairs — as soon as I open a tin, he'll come like a rocket."

"I need to text my mom."

"Got it."

As he headed downstairs, Melody took out her phone and texted: "Checking in. What's your ETA?"

From downstairs, she heard James say, "Buster? Where you at, buddy?"

A few seconds later, Melody saw a grey cone-wearing figure dash across the entry hall and head down the stairs.

Her phone vibrated with a message from her mom: "There in half an hour."

She texted back: "See you soon! Drive safely!"

She was about to head downstairs to help James when he appeared with the cat crate, Buster safely inside. The cat peered out at her and gave her another plaintive *meow*.

"You'll be home soon, Buster," she said.

James said, "Got everything you need?"

"I think so."

He seemed serious now, like he was figuring out a battle plan. "When we head out, I'll drive in the lead and you follow. Stay behind me on the drive into town so you can see if I run into icy patches."

"Got it."

She opened the door and watched James head toward his SUV. She flipped off the light and shut the door behind her.

The freezing rain was coming down heavily now. There was something so relentless about it, so inexorable, like the storm knew what it was doing and was in no mood to stop.

Wrapping her coat around her neck, she carefully made her way to her SUV and hopped in. She heard the sound of James's SUV starting up, then watched as he backed out, turned around, and pulled up next to her. Through the window, she saw him give her a thumb's up and say, "You ready?"

She returned the thumb's up and followed him as he headed out. They reached the trees, slowly winding their way down the gravel driveway toward Summit Lane.

Later, when she thought back on the moment that followed, she realized she heard what happened before she saw it. A sharp crack echoed through the trees, followed immediately by a sudden movement — of something shockingly big — falling in front of James's SUV. James hit his brakes hard as she heard a crash and felt a ground-shaking thud.

With a gasp, Melody slammed on her brakes. The SUV slid several feet before mercifully coming to a stop.

Heart pounding, she watched James jump out of

his SUV, look toward her to make sure she was okay, then run up ahead.

When he didn't immediately return, Melody found herself unbuckling and stepping out and running after him.

Oh, it was cold. And so wet! Freezing rain splattered over her face. The sound of the falling rain filled the air around her.

Then she saw it and gasped.

A huge branch had fallen across the gravel driveway.

James was bent over and pulling at it, trying to see how heavy it was, grunting as he tried to move it.

"Let me help," she said, joining him.

She reached down and gripped it, surprised by how thick the branch was — easily as thick as her leg.

"One, two, three," he said, and then —

Melody pulled with all her might, James straining next to her — and the branch barely budged.

A second loud crack racketed through the woods and Melody gasped again. Up ahead, through the heavy rain, another branch crashed to the ground.

James stood up. "We need to get our cars out of the woods and back to the house. Are you okay driving in reverse?"

"Yes," she said.

"After you."

Melody didn't need encouraging. Heart pounding, she hurried back to her SUV, slipped into reverse, and carefully eased back through the trees. When she reached the open meadow, she exhaled with relief, then watched anxiously until James made it out as well.

Shaking from the realization of how close they'd come to being hit by falling branches, she pulled once again in front of the house.

James hopped out of his SUV and approached. Willing herself to calm down, she rolled down her window.

"What do you need from your SUV?" he said.

He'd reached the same conclusion she had, obviously.

She reached into her pocket and handed him her house key. "You get Buster inside."

He nodded and returned to his SUV. Working together, they gathered up what they needed and headed back inside. It was with a sense of relief that Melody once again closed the door behind them.

They were both dripping wet, and inside the crate, an annoyed cat was *meowing* furiously.

But the most important thing was: *They were safe.*

And also, she realized with a jolt:

They were stuck!

CHAPTER 16

*M*elody's stomach clenched as the reality of the situation sank in. Her mom and Benny were due to arrive any minute.

And if she wasn't there to greet them....

James had said her name, she realized. "Melody," he repeated.

She blinked as she returned to the moment. "Sorry, yes?"

"Does your dryer work? Has it been installed?"

Her dryer? Her new washer and dryer were located in a closet one floor up, next to the bedrooms on the second floor. But had she seen them during her quick house tour earlier?

"I don't know," she confessed. "I think so? But I'm not sure, because I didn't open that door."

"I'll check. We should dry off. The towels are soaking wet."

"Yes, of course."

He set the cat crate down and opened the latch. Immediately, an annoyed Buster rushed out and dashed off.

"Poor fellow," Melody murmured.

"I'll make it up to him." James took off his wet jacket, then picked up the soaked towels that were acting as a temporary doormat. "How about we get your coat and gloves into the dryer, too?"

Yes, she thought. "Thank you." She shrugged out of them and handed them to him.

"Up one floor?" he asked.

"Next to the bathroom."

And then he was off, taking the stairs in confident strides.

Cold water tickled her scalp — her hair was sopping wet. With an impatient tug, she unfastened her ponytail and bent over, running her fingers through her hair to encourage the water to fall away from her skin.

Had she left anything in her coat pockets? She checked her jeans and was relieved to find her phone in it.

The thought came: *Clara!*

She whipped out her phone and dialed Clara. Thankfully, she heard the phone ringing. She almost cried out with relief when she heard her friend's familiar voice.

"Melody, what's up?"

"Darling, I can't tell you how glad I am to reach you."

"Is something wrong?" Clara said, voice rising.

"We're stuck up at the house."

"Stuck? We?"

"James and I. Branches have fallen and are blocking the driveway."

"How many branches, do you know? And how big?"

"At least one. We tried moving it, but it's too heavy."

"Are you two okay?"

"Yes, darling, we're inside the house, safe and sound."

"And your cars?"

"Both fine as well. Were you able to find a battery for the big saw?"

"No," Clara said, her frustration evident. "We've got smaller saws, so we'll get through this, but it'll take longer, that's all."

"Can you add us to the branch-clearing list?"

"Of course."

"Any idea how long it will take to head our way?"

"Right now, can't say for sure. We're getting reports of fallen branches from all over, and the freezing rain is still coming down. We have to prioritize the main roads and life-threatening situations."

"Darling, give me your honest answer. How long do you think it will be?"

After a pause, Clara said, "You might be stuck there overnight."

Melody swallowed back her disappointment. Somehow, she'd known that was going to be the answer. "My mom and Benny are due at the Inn any minute."

"I'll call the Inn and let them know the situation."

"I should call them now, too."

"Yes, you should. You don't know how long you'll have power and phone service."

A surge of panic rose within her — she hadn't even considered the storm's other implications — but she immediately pushed the emotion down. "These ice storms are no joke, are they?"

"No, they are not. You call your mom. I'll make sure Barbara and Stu at the Inn know the deal."

"Thank you, darling." She felt herself tremble. "See you … tomorrow?"

"If not sooner. You take care up there."

Melody heard Clara hang up. At that moment, she heard a faint low rumble from upstairs — the sound of a dryer being turned on.

At least *that* was going their way. Curious, she made her way upstairs, where she found James in the hallway in front of the dryer, staring at his phone.

"I don't have a signal," he said. "You get through?"

"I talked to Clara. Told her we're stuck."

"Would you mind if I called Anna and let her know?"

"Of course."

She was handing him her phone when it vibrated. She looked down: *Her mom!*

"Mom!" she said, picking up. "Where are you?"

"We just arrived at the Inn," her mom said.

"Thank goodness," Melody said, relief flooding through her. "Are you and Benny okay?"

"Safe and sound."

"So glad to hear. Any troubles on the road?"

"The last few miles were a bit scary — I'll give you that," her mom said with a small laugh. "The storm came from out of nowhere. But Benny took it slow. There was a car in front us that we were able to follow."

"I'm so glad you made it safely."

"Where are you right now?"

"Up at the new house."

"Are you heading down soon?"

Melody swallowed. "Unfortunately, no, at least not right away. We're stuck."

"Stuck, dear?" There was alarm in her mom's voice. "Are you okay?"

"Oh, we're fine. It's just that there are tree branches down and the road is blocked. So for now, I'm camped out at the new house."

"Camped out?"

"Nothing to worry about. The house has heat and electricity and hot water — it's all good."

"How long do you think you'll be up there?"

"I'm not sure, but possibly overnight. Is Barbara there?"

"Yes, she's right here. Would you like to speak with her?"

"Yes, that would be great."

After a second, Melody heard Barbara's familiar voice.

"Melody, did I hear right? You're stuck up at your new house?"

"That's right. I'm here with James — James Newcastle. We're fine — no emergencies or anything like that — but branches have fallen across the road and we can't get out. Can you call James's daughter Anna and let her know her dad's stuck up here but everything's okay?"

"Of course."

"Clara's going to call you as well. I spoke with her briefly. She knows we'll need help with branch clearing, but she said we're probably stuck here till tomorrow."

"Got it. Are you sure you're okay up there?"

"I'm fine. We're fine. The house has electricity and heat and a working fireplace."

"What about food?"

Food, Melody realized. *Pretty slim pickings on that front.* But there was no point in telling Barbara that.

"No fears, darling. We have more than enough to see us through."

"Okay, good. And listen, I have news. Big news. About a half an hour ago, I got the surprise of my life when —"

Barbara's voice cut off — suddenly and abruptly.

Melody frowned.

She looked at her phone, then brought it back to her ear. "Barbara? Barbara? Are you there? Can you hear me?"

The line was silent.

Their connection was *gone*.

Which meant:

Now they truly were cut off.

She swallowed back another surge of emotion. It didn't feel real, somehow — what was happening at this very moment seemed like a story she was being told about someone else — yet real it was.

She glanced at James and found him gazing at her with concern. "No more phone?"

"Apparently not," she said, trying to quell her unease. "Barbara was in the middle of telling me she'd just had the surprise of her life. But before she could say what, the line went dead."

He looked at his own phone, then shook his head. "Still nothing." He exhaled. "Thank you for asking Barbara to call Anna."

"I'm sorry you weren't able to talk with her and check up on her."

"She's working at the bookstore today, and our house is only a couple of blocks away, so she's fine. I just didn't want her worrying about me."

"Speaking of worrying, I'm so glad my mom and Benny made it to the Inn safely."

"I'm glad about that, too."

They looked at each other for a moment, the rumble of the dryer filling the silence, the reality of their situation sinking in.

"Well," she said awkwardly, "I guess we're going to be here awhile."

"Looks like."

She clapped her hands together, trying to banish the awkwardness and replace it with confidence.

"So what do we do now?"

$\mathcal{S}$he was asking a good question, she realized. A very good question.

When a storm strikes and one gets stuck in an empty house with a stranger, what does one do?

"Well," James said, apparently taking her question seriously. "We should do an inventory. Figure out what we have."

"Great idea," she said, immediately warming to the idea.

"Especially while we still have power."

Yes, power. Clara had mentioned that as well. Clearly, these locals operated on the same wavelength when it came to storms.

"I bought candles at the hardware store," she said, suddenly remembering. "And a lighter!"

"Good," he said, then pointed to her wet boots. "How are your socks?"

"Damp," she said, noticing for the first time that his boots were off and his feet were bare.

"We should pop them in the dryer."

"Of course." She bent down and slid out of her winter boots, then took off her socks, opened the dryer door, and tossed them in. "I've never had my own washer-dryer," she said as she admired her brand-new stacked washer-dryer and its gleaming chrome curves. "Even when I was growing up. And my apartment in New York is too small."

"You have a good one now. Okay, let's see what else we have."

Together, they made their way downstairs. The wood floor felt cool on her bare feet — she'd welcome having her socks back as soon as they were dry — but she was pleased to discover that the floor didn't feel *cold*.

"The heating system seems to be working," she said as she stepped past damp spots in the entry hall.

James picked up the bag of snacks she'd impulsively purchased at the gas station. "You put in radiant heating under the floors, right?"

"Yes, on every level."

"Between that and the forced-air heating and the fireplace, you're pretty well set up."

"I remember Luke telling me about the heating plan," Melody said, recalling how enthusiastic he'd been about the various details and technical specs and what-not — way more enthusiastic than she'd been listening to him, if she was being honest with herself. Now, months later, with her bare feet relying on the new system he'd been so excited to install, she realized she owed him a silent apology. "It's some kind of new-fangled smart heating system — energy-efficient and self-adjusting and precise and I don't know what else."

"It's a good night to put it to the test."

As they made their way down the entry hall, Melody considered how she felt about the turn of events that had led to this moment. Getting trapped in an isolated house in a storm with a man she barely knew was *not* something she'd ever expected would happen to her. The inconvenience was indisputable, her anxiety was understandable, and — the thought came unbidden — she had every right to feel nervous and even alarmed.

And yet … with James, she wasn't feeling alarmed, and her instincts were generally accurate on this score. This fellow, she sensed, was one of the good ones.

Ahead of her, James pushed through the swinging door into the kitchen. Melody's hand found the light switch and flipped it on.

James paused for a moment, taking it in. "Nice job with the lighting in here."

She had to concur. A row of overhead light

fixtures — globes of frosted glass, positioned above the spot where her long kitchen work table would soon rest — cast a warm glow. Additional lighting beneath the upper cabinets and over the stove meant she'd always have the right amount of light for whatever task was at hand.

"My architect Teddy dabbles in lighting for off-Broadway shows," she said.

"Broadway," James repeated. "We were talking about that when we got distracted back at the tree farm. Is Broadway where you met Teddy?"

"We were both involved in the same off-Broadway production, six years ago. He was doing lighting and production design and probably a half-dozen other jobs as well — it's like that in smaller productions — and I had a supporting role. My first significant role, by the way."

"What had you done before that?"

"You mean, besides study and struggle and audition and audition and audition and never get cast?"

He gave her a smile. "The role was a step up?"

"A big step up. I had lines — actual lines! — and a solo song."

"Had you been cast in any roles before that?"

"In the chorus, in several productions."

"Ah."

"I'll always be grateful for that little show — even though it was a supporting role in an off-Broadway play and barely paid."

"And that's because…."

"A casting director came to one of the shows and saw something in me. She suggested I audition for an upcoming play — a big production, on Broadway, the real deal — so I did and got the part and … one thing led to another."

He was regarding her steadily. "It takes hard work, doesn't it? Perseverance, determination, a willingness to keep at it even when things aren't going your way…."

"Especially when things aren't going your way."

"Plus talent."

"And a good dose of luck."

"Because life isn't always fair?"

"The universe isn't a level playing field. It's important to be prepared. When luck hits, you have to be ready for it. Some of us have to work harder and travel further to achieve our dreams."

She realized with a start that the conversation had suddenly gotten rather serious, even personal. James seemed to realize that — or perhaps something in her expression had given her away — because he turned his attention back to the kitchen.

"So," he said. "Your architect friend Teddy. Is the kitchen his design?"

"Yes, with help from Luke and me. Teddy and Luke figured out the layout — where the fridge and sink should go, and how to rework the hearth, where the electrical outlets should be placed, things like that. And then Teddy and I focused on the finishing touches."

"The three of you did a great job." He set the bag on the counter, then gestured to the center of the room. "I assume you'll put a table here?"

"A country-style work table."

He nodded with approval. "Sounds great."

"It's beautiful and sturdy and exactly what I wanted for this space." She gestured to the bags of goods piled on the counters. "Let's see what we have."

Together, they started unloading the bags from the hardware store, spreading the various items out on the counter to get a sense of what they had.

"Glad you got candles and a lighter," he said. "And a flashlight."

"I wish I'd gotten more towels," she said with a sigh. "We could use them."

"The ones upstairs will be dry soon enough."

She'd done pretty well with the cleaning equipment and supplies — she was well-covered when it came to brooms and paper towels and the like. But there were glaring gaps, especially when it came to kitchen basics.

"How are we going to boil water?" she said out loud.

James swept his gaze over the assembled items. "Good question. I don't see a kettle...."

"Or even a pan," she sighed. *Urgh.* How could

she have missed something so essential? She was a homeowner now; she needed to start acting like one. It was time to step up her game and start channeling her inner Clara. From this moment on, she was going to start writing down actual lists, using actual words to represent actual items that she actually needed.

James went to the tap and turned it on. "At least we have hot water," he said after a few seconds, his finger under the running water. "Nice and hot. Though not anything to drink the water in...."

She inhaled sharply — *he was right*. No mugs. No glasses. She hadn't even bought disposable paper cups!

"Wait," she said, remembering. "I have a latte cup from the cafe this morning. I brought it in with me. I must have set it down somewhere...."

"We'll find it. And I have a thermos downstairs."

She sighed. "James, I'm sorry about this. If I'd been thinking more clearly, I would have realized how poorly prepared I was and done something about it."

He shook his head. "No need to apologize. There's no way you could have anticipated this happening. I've been through storms like this before, and even I didn't expect this much rain to fall and freeze so fast."

"It's nice of you to say, but it doesn't change the fact that my new house is not very welcoming right now."

He gestured to the final unpacked bag — her impulsive gas station purchases. "I'm dying to see what's on the menu for dinner tonight."

He had a small grin on his face as he said it, prompting a smile of her own.

"Darling," she said, "prepare yourself for a high-end feast."

Quickly, she unpacked the bag and laid out the items on the counter.

An assortment of candy bars. Instant popcorn. Beef jerky. Red licorice. Instant hot chocolate.

"It's like I'm ten years old again," he said.

"That's so true!" she said with a laugh.

"Perfect for a camping trip."

"If only we had marshmallows and graham crackers and chocolate."

"Mmmm, s'mores," he said, then gestured behind her. "What's that over there?"

She turned and gasped. *The box of treats from the cafe!*

She grabbed it and opened it, almost deliriously glad to see — and inhale the aroma of— the scones and muffins that Holly had so thoughtfully provided.

"From the cafe?" James said.

"Holly gave them to me this morning. She just became my new favorite person ever."

James chuckled. "Looks like we'll be just fine in the food department."

"You know," she said, feeling relieved and oddly elated, "I think you're right."

"So we should probably get to the next part of our inventory," he said.

"The next part?"

"Figuring out our sleeping arrangements."

CHAPTER 18

*A*h, yes — sleeping arrangements. But there were no beds! No furniture at all, in fact. Just —

"I noticed two couches in the living room," James said, taking the words out of her mouth.

Luke had mentioned the couches that morning, but she hadn't even seen them yet, because she hadn't even been in her new living room yet! "Everything else is coming tomorrow," she said, then glanced out the kitchen window, where the freezing rain showed no signs of letting up. "Assuming the storm lets us, of course."

They made their way back down the hallway, then turned left at the stairs and into her new living area. She'd already seen photos, but she couldn't keep a smile from her lips as she gazed upon the room in person for the first time. It was a large, open space, currently empty except for two big matching couches, clad in a soft neutral mocha chenille fabric, in the center of the room. A big fireplace ran along one wall, with floor-to-ceiling windows along the outside wall facing the back of the property. When the weather was better, the view of the valley would be spectacular.

The radiant floor heat warmed her toes, but what touched her heart was the care that Luke and his team had clearly taken with the finishing touches. As her gaze roved over the room, it seemed that everything — the hardwood flooring, the wood-paneled walls, the recessed lighting in the ceiling with its warm glow — was perfect.

She stepped toward the big stone fireplace, her hand moving toward the thick wood mantel, her fingers lightly tracing the subtle curves of the wood. "Beautiful," she murmured.

She realized James had gone silent. She turned to find him gazing at her, seemingly pleased and embarrassed at the same time, and realized —

"This is your work, isn't it?" she said, nodding toward the mantel.

"That's right."

"It's stunning."

"Thanks."

He seemed shy suddenly — as if the confidence he exuded in other respects had temporarily vanished. Why was that? She wanted to find out, but her instincts told her to ease in. "Tell me about this piece of wood."

His shoulders relaxed, as if relieved to shift the focus away from himself. "Old-growth cedar. Reclaimed from an old barn not too far from here. The wood is well over a century old. It's the same wood as your dining table."

"You picked wonderfully. The proportions are perfect for this big old fireplace." She ran her fingers over the mantel's outer edge, which wasn't cut in a straight line, but rather seemed to flow with the grains of the wood. "What's this technique called?"

"Live edge."

"I love how it looks and feels."

"Glad you like it."

"How do you know if a piece of wood is right for this technique?"

His brow furrowed as he considered her question. "I guess I just know. In the case of the mantel, I knew what the fireplace looked like and how big it was and the room it was in, so I had a general sense of what I was after."

"But knowing you found the right piece…. Is that a gut-level thing?"

"Very much so," he said, his grey eyes seeming to intensify. "When I find what I'm after, I know right away."

A flutter of pleasure rippled through her, which she promptly pushed down. There was a strong jaw beneath that trimmed brown beard. The hair on his head looked thick and full.

Both of which were totally irrelevant to their conversation. They were talking about woodworking, after all.

A piece of cedar.

Right?

A realization dawned — and with it a wave of self-consciousness — about a decision she'd made that morning. A decision she'd made so lightly, so easily, without any regard for possible consequences.

A decision she hadn't considered for a second — until now.

Namely: *She was wearing no makeup!* Not a lick. What did her face look like, after being caught in a storm and getting soaked in freezing rain?

And her hair — *oh, dear.* What had she been thinking when she'd loosened her ponytail to let her hair dry faster? How in the world had she failed to take into account her hair's untamable desire to run wild when left untended?

Why had these essential realities eluded her until now? Why, why, *why?*

Poor James, she realized with dismay, was now looking at a wild-haired, pale-faced *mess.*

So much for putting her best face forward!

"Let's start a fire," she said, suddenly desperately eager to be doing something — anything — to turn their attention toward something else.

James, bless his heart, didn't seem to notice her inner turmoil, or at least pretended not to. Taking her cue, he pointed to a button on the wall next to the mantel. "May I?"

"Please."

He pressed the button and, with a soft *whoosh*, the fireplace roared to life.

As the first flames appeared, she felt herself calming. There was nothing she could do about her face, she told herself, giving her practical-minded inner Clara a try. When she had a spare moment, she'd find a mirror — assuming she had a mirror in this place, she realized, recalling the lack of wall cabinets above the bathroom sinks — to confirm that nothing too terrible was going on. If need be, she could run out to the car and check her face in the rear-view mirror. Besides, she was probably overreacting. There were no paparazzi here to catch her in a bad-photo moment. Just this fellow James, who didn't seem to mind how she looked. In fact, if she was reading the subtle signals right, he seemed to be enjoying looking at her.

No, she ordered herself. *Do not go there.* Better to focus on her new fireplace, which really was quite lovely, even soothing. The flames flickering up from the faux logs were pumping out lovely heat and bathing her toes in warmth.

"I'm glad you went with gas instead of wood," James said. "Especially on a night like tonight."

"I originally wanted wood-burning," she said, recalling the debate she'd had with Luke. "I wanted to respect the house and its history and stay traditional. I had a vision of me chopping wood out back and bringing logs in for the fire and watching them slowly crackle and burn...."

"I sense a but...."

"But Luke talked me out of it. He said gas was better, and that wood-burning was more work to maintain and not as efficient and caused more pollution."

"So now that you're here and looking at the actual thing, what's the verdict?"

"It's quite lovely," she said. "And quite...."

Romantic, she almost said. Which was *not* a word she wanted to use at this particular moment.

"Appropriate," she finally said. "The fire looks like a wood-burning fire. In terms of appearance, it could be a fire from a century ago."

"Agreed," he said, kneeling down to warm his hands. "It looks right and feels right. And the heat is right."

As she gazed upon his strong hands, she realized a lot of things in this moment were right.

Which was just her being silly. She barely knew this man. The smart course of action was to move past her concerns about her appearance, stop noticing *his* appearance, and get back to doing something productive.

With a decisiveness she almost felt, she turned toward the two couches. "I guess this is where we'll be sleeping. Maybe we can push them closer to the fire?"

He nodded. "Makes sense."

Without needing to say more, they moved them into position facing each other about four feet apart in front of the fireplace. Even though they were both grownups and the sleeping situation was obvious and clear, there was still something awkward about the moment.

James said, "I don't suppose you have blankets anywhere?"

"Unfortunately, no. I ordered bedding for each bed, but none of it's here yet."

"Anything in your SUV?"

She thought a second, then shook her head. "Stu and I unloaded everything I brought up from New York, so all of that's at the Inn. Should I start keeping a blanket in the car at all times, in case of emergency?"

He nodded. "Can't hurt. The thing is, I don't have one right now either. Mine's in the wash back home. I picked the wrong day to clean it. At least we'll have our coats and the towels when they're done drying."

"Don't forget our socks!"

He grinned. "And our socks." Then his eyes lit up. "I have an idea."

"For blankets?"

"Sort of. Want to see what I have in mind?"

He looked rather adorable standing there, waiting for her response. He seemed genuinely interested in making her feel comfortable.

He cocked his head to the side, and she realized he was waiting for her to answer.

Because she'd gotten distracted and hadn't answered yet.

Which wouldn't do!

"Of course!" she said. "I'm all yours."

CHAPTER 19

All yours? she almost growled to herself. *Really?* Of all the words she could have used, she'd picked *those two*? Surely a simple *okay* or *sounds fine* would have sufficed. Or even the ever-handy *yes.*

Thankfully, James hadn't seemed to notice. "Follow me," he said, then headed for the stairs that led down to the media room. "There might be sawdust or chips on the floor," he added as she hurried after him, "so watch where you step."

Indeed, as she descended the stairs, she felt the grainy, dusty texture of sawdust clinging to her toes.

"I usually run a vacuum when I'm done for the day," he said, "but today...."

"Today you were interrupted by the new home-owner and her dangerous quest for a Christmas tree."

He shot her a grin, then pointed to the tarp beneath the work table. "I'm thinking we can use these."

She focused in and realized he'd laid not one, but two canvas floor coverings beneath the table.

"For … blankets?" she said.

"What do you think?"

She shrugged, dubious. "It's worth a try."

He picked up one end of the table, raising two of the table legs off the floor. "If you could…."

"Got it," she said as she reached down and pulled the tarp out from under the table legs.

After doing the same at the other end of the table, James grabbed a tarp and gently shook it, sending a cascade of sawdust and wood chips to the floor.

"Sorry about the dust," he said.

"Oh, I'm fine with sawdust. Carpenters are the unsung heroes of the Broadway stage."

After a few more increasingly vigorous shakes, he folded the tarp and handed it to her. "Your substitute blanket."

"Thank you." She stepped back and watched him shake and then fold the second tarp. The canvas felt rough, but his idea was a good one — the tarp had a thickness that would probably help when it came to staying warm. "Anything you need before we go back up?"

"Just my thermos."

She spied it on the floor next to his toolbox and grabbed it. "Got it."

After pausing at the foot of the stairs to brush the sawdust from her feet, she made her way up, James close behind.

"I wonder where Buster went to," she said.

"He'll be back when he's ready to hang out. Or when he's hungry. Or both."

"Speaking of food," she said as she set her so-called blanket next to her couch.

"You hungry?"

"Ravenous. I haven't eaten anything since this morning."

His eyebrows went up. "You need a scone."

Her stomach rumbled at the thought. "Lead the way."

It was then, as they reached the kitchen, that the lights suddenly went out. In a blink, the warm glow vanished, replaced by a murky darkness.

"Oh, my," she said.

Blocked from leaving, no phone service, and now — *no power.*

As her eyes adjusted, she saw James — or his shadow, at least — step toward the counter.

A few seconds later, he said, "Found the flashlight. I saw batteries earlier."

"Next to the flashlight."

"Thanks." A few seconds later, she heard him rip open the battery package, unscrew the flashlight, drop in batteries, and screw the flashlight back up. It was interesting to listen to it all happen. Although she couldn't see a thing in the darkness, each sound was clearly identifiable.

With a soft click, the flashlight blazed on.

"Here you go," he said, handing her the light.

"Thank you." The light's heft felt good. Just knowing she had it made her feel better.

He clapped his hands together. "How about we take the food into the living room? A picnic in front of the fire?"

She smiled — she liked the way he described it. "Sounds perfect."

"I should get the clothes out of the dryer."

"Why don't you do that and I'll take care of the food?"

"See you at the campsite."

And with that, he was gone. She nearly called out to ask if he needed the light, then stopped herself. He knew what he was doing. Presumably, if he felt he needed the flashlight, he would have asked for it. Perhaps he was part owl, with excellent night vision?

She gathered the box of scones and gas-station snacks into her arms, then pushed through the swinging door and returned to the living room, the flickering fire drawing her back. She set the food down in the empty space between the two sofas and sighed.

She was thirsty, she realized. Where had she left

her latte cup? She'd set it down somewhere — but where?

Time to put the flashlight to work. If the cup wasn't in the kitchen, then it had to be in one of the other rooms she'd been in earlier.

With the beam lighting her path, she made her way upstairs, where James was slipping into his socks in front of the dryer.

"How did the dryer do?" she asked.

He handed her her socks. "See for yourself."

Her fingers touched warm wool and she gasped, "Oh, my." Setting the flashlight down, she slipped into one sock and then the other. The heat on her toes felt *marvelous*. "Darling, my feet are in heaven."

He chuckled. "Ditto."

"I came up in search of my latte cup."

"Ah."

"I'm retracing my steps."

"I can join, if you'd like."

"No, I can manage. Why don't you take the clothes downstairs?"

"See you in a bit."

Before she could change her mind, she headed up the stairs to the attic level and then up the spiral stairs to the top of the tower, retracing her steps from that morning.

When she reached the tower room, she aimed the beam around the space, quickly determining that the cup wasn't there. But instead of heading down right away, she found herself lingering, drawn by the steady thrum of the falling rain. She turned off the flashlight and once again allowed her eyes to adjust. Goodness, it was dark outside. Only gradually was she able to make out shapes below. In front of the house, the two SUVs came into view, and past them the open ground of the meadow, the woods beyond a shapeless dark blur.

The falling rain sounded peaceful and unlike anything she could ever hope to hear in New York, where a cacophony of sounds constantly competed for attention. Up here, in her adopted home, it was like she was experiencing an all-natural noise-cancelling machine.

A thought came: James would start worrying if she dawdled for too long. He was like that, she sensed — a natural protector. After a final glance around, she slipped back down the spiral staircase, then hurried across the open attic toward her new bathroom.

She frowned when she didn't find the cup. There was only one more spot it could be. With a sigh of appreciation — she really had nailed the design in this room — she made her way down to the second floor.

There, in the large bedroom, on the floor next to the work table with the wallpaper samples, she found her latte cup.

"Victory," she whispered.

Quickly, she made her way back to James, her anticipation rising for whatever might come next.

CHAPTER 20

S
he found him laying a tarp-blanket on her couch.

He glanced over as she arrived. "Success?"

She held up the cup. "Success."

"Good." He pointed to the tarp. "If you wrap the tarp around you like a sleeping bag, I think it'll help you keep warm."

She stepped closer to the fire to let the heat seep into her socks. "Does the power go out often?"

He shrugged. "Not often. We haven't had an ice storm in over a decade. A few years ago, a blizzard caused temporary outages."

"I'm glad the gas is unaffected."

"If we didn't have the fire and hot water, we really would be camping."

She picked up her winter coat, now toasty warm

from the dryer, and slipped it on, sighing in contentment as she was enveloped in a cocoon of heat. "Darling, this coat feels marvelous."

He gestured to the food on the floor. "Shall we?"

With a nod, she sank to the floor and opened the box of scones. "Mind if I...?"

"By all means."

"Do you have a favorite?"

"All of them are great — Holly doesn't do a bad scone — but I like her cranberry-apple the best."

"I had one this morning, at the cafe with Clara and Luke. That seems so long ago — like a million things have happened since."

She reached in and picked a scone at random, bringing it close and discovering a lovely aroma of bacon and apple. "This one has bacon. Do you mind?"

He sat across from her and said, "Dig in."

She took a bite and nearly cried out with pleasure. *My, she was hungry!* How had she not noticed sooner? Back in New York, during long rehearsals, she often went long stretches without eating, but only because she was completely immersed in bringing a theatrical production to life. Surely today's activities — exploring and shopping and escaping a storm — couldn't compare?

Or could they? The tastes of apple and bacon delighted her senses as the question rolled through her. If she hadn't given food even a second's thought all day — and she hadn't — then did that mean she'd been fully engaged in what she'd been doing? On some level, was it fair and reasonable to conclude that she'd actually *enjoyed* today's cavalcade of events?

"Penny for your thoughts," James said.

She blinked, startled.

"I'm thirsty," she said, surprising herself again.

He pointed to the hot chocolate. "How about we give that a try?"

"Will the water coming out of the tap be hot enough?"

"Only one way to find out."

He stood up, grabbing the hot chocolate box and his thermos, and she scrambled to follow, pausing only to grab her empty latte cup and the flashlight.

"You don't need any light?" she said. "Are you part owl or something?"

"Ha — I wish." At the sink, he rinsed his thermos, then stood aside while she did the same with her cup.

She watched him rip open a packet and tap the powdered mix into his thermos.

He turned on the hot water and waited a few seconds for it to heat up. "Moment of truth," he said, then filled his thermos with hot water.

Almost immediately, the familiar aroma of chocolate reached her. He gave the thermos a shake to speed up the dissolving, then brought it to his lips for a taste.

She could see his face, thanks to the flashlight beam aimed at the ceiling. He was pursing his lips, his face a study in concentration.

"Well?" she said, her anticipation building.

"Give it a try," he said, handing her the thermos.

She brought it to her nose. Maybe it was the circumstances, maybe her hunger and thirst, but the aroma was incredibly enticing — comfortable and irresistible all at once.

Her sip confirmed it: The instant hot chocolate, a mass-market product bought at a gas station and mixed with not-quite-boiling water, was a *winner*.

"Mmm," she said. "Don't tell my gourmet friends in New York, but this is delicious."

James chuckled. "Totally hits the spot."

Quickly, she added a packet to her cup and filled it with hot water.

"Not even a spoon to stir with," she sighed. "I can't believe how many basics I forgot to buy."

"Give it a swirl — that'll do the trick."

The cup was so warm in her hands. The aroma of the hot chocolate — so welcoming. The man standing in front of her — so attentive.

But this James Newcastle was still a stranger. She suddenly knew she wanted to change that.

"Tell me about yourself," she said.

He blinked, momentarily taken aback. "Happy to.

What do you want to know?" He gestured toward the living room. "How about we get back to the fire?"

She nodded her agreement. "I do know a few things about you," she said as they left the kitchen. "I know you're a dad with a great daughter, I know you design your own furniture, I know you do wood-working jobs. But I feel like there's a lot more to know about James Newcastle."

They settled onto their couches in front of the fire.

"Tell me what you think of your tarp blanket," he said with a smile.

She set her cup on the floor and arranged the tarp over her feet. It crinkled as she adjusted it, but as she got it wrapped around her, she sensed it would work rather well.

"This is going to be just fine."

"Good. Also," he added, tossing her a towel, "I figure we can fold these up to use as pillows."

She smiled. "There's something else I know about you."

"Oh, what's that?"

"You're good at taking care of people."

He shrugged but didn't reply, as if the compliment made him self-conscious.

"Like earlier. You knew I needed help with the Christmas tree, so you volunteered to come with me."

He took a deep breath. "I didn't want to impose,

or have you think I was assuming you couldn't do it yourself…."

"But you sensed — correctly — that this New York City girl was out of her depth. Which I very much was. So thank you for offering."

He regarded her steadily. "Glad I was able to help."

She was glad, too. A distance of four feet, maybe five, separated their couches. The flickering light of the fire cast a soft glow over his features. He lay on his side facing her, his long legs beneath his tarp blanket, his hand holding his thermos of hot chocolate.

There was no ring on the third finger of his left hand — had she noticed that earlier?

"I assume you were — are — married?" she asked, pleased to hear the question leave her mouth in a carefully neutral manner.

"Divorced," he said. "Eight years now."

"What happened, if you don't mind my asking?"

"I don't mind at all." He shifted into an upright position. "My ex Tammy and I were young when we got married — too young. I was twenty, she was nineteen. Still kids, really. Neither of us knew a thing about life or had a clue what we wanted."

Melody nodded, remembering herself at that age and how much she still had to learn.

He continued. "It became pretty clear pretty fast that we weren't the right fit. We had different temperaments, different likes, different dislikes, different goals — you name it, we weren't in sync. But we did our best to stay together for Anna's sake. It was only after a decade of trying that we finally accepted that it wasn't working."

"That's when you divorced?"

He nodded. "Not a happy time. A fair amount of anger and resentment, both of us hurting." He swallowed. "But through it all, I will say this: We did our best to keep our arguments away from Anna. Both of us did our best to be good parents."

"Where's your ex now?"

"In Eagle Cove, the next town over, across the lake. She remarried about five years ago. She and her husband have a daughter of their own. Anna's half-sister."

"How do you feel about that?"

"I'm happy for them. Their daughter Lacey is three now — a real sweet kid. And Tammy and Ed — that's her husband's name — are a good couple. Way better than Tammy and I ever were. Plus, he's a good guy."

"So how do you two get along now?"

"It's better now. The tension's gone. When we run into each other or when we speak, everything's good. I think it helps that, even when things were toughest, we were always able to find common ground when it came to Anna."

"Any regrets?"

"Sure," he said without hesitation. "If I could go back and fix the past, there's stuff I'd change in a heartbeat. But we can't do that, can we?"

"No," she murmured, her mind tumbling backward. "We can't."

"The value of mistakes is what we learn from them."

She liked his words — they resonated. "I agree."

"Not just learn from them," he said, sitting up straighter. "Also what we *gain* from them. Mistakes can be blessings. The greatest gift in my life — my daughter — wouldn't have happened if Tammy and I hadn't made the mistakes we made."

She'd been right — she definitely wanted to learn more about this James Newcastle.

She cast her mind back to the previous evening. The young woman she'd met at the bookstore seemed smart, friendly, cheerful, and confident — brimming with life. All of which suggested she'd been raised by loving parents.

She took a sip, the chocolate warming her. "I still can't get over the fact that the wonderful young woman I met last night is your daughter. She seems amazing."

"She's the light of my life." His eyes glistened with sudden emotion. "I'm so proud of her."

Melody felt a tug. He seemed so *real*. "What year is she in college?"

"Sophomore year. Studying history. She's

thinking about graduate school, getting a Ph.D., becoming a professor."

"What kind of history?"

"Right now she's taking all sorts of classes, but her interest is in the history of this region."

"New England has such a rich history."

"She had a project last semester that required original research. She came home for a weekend and spent two days rooting through the town library and church records, looking for birth records relating to the town's founders."

"Did she find what she was looking for?"

He grinned. "Tons of interesting stuff."

"Like what?"

"What do you know about the town's founders, the Heartsprings family?"

"Not much. Bits and pieces."

"The town was founded in the 1700s by a lumber merchant named Jedediah Heartsprings. His last known descendant, a wonderful lady named Minerva Heartsprings, passed away a few years back."

"I've heard about her," Melody said. "Didn't she use to live in the old Victorian that's now the veterinary clinic?"

"That's right. That's her."

"So Anna learned something about Minerva's family?"

"That's right." He smiled, his pride in his daughter's achievement clear. "Everyone thought the Heartsprings clan died out with Minerva."

Melody's eyebrows rose. "But…?"

"Anna discovered a branch still alive and kicking."

"Oh, my!"

"None of that branch lives here — they're all out West."

"Who are they descended from?"

"Minerva's great-great-uncle, a fellow named Abraham Heartsprings, who went to California in 1849 in search of gold and never came back."

"What does this discovery mean for the town?"

"That's what folks are trying to figure out. Anna presented her research to the town council, and now they're talking about reaching out to Abraham's descendants and inviting them to Heartsprings Valley for a celebration of the town's history."

Melody sat up. "That's the thing about this town."

"What do you mean?"

"Heartsprings Valley knows its history. Not only that, it honors it and celebrates it. Not every place can say that in this day and age."

"So true," he said. "Now, if you don't mind, I'd like to turn the tables."

"In what way?" she said, surprised.

"I think it's time for me to learn more about the history of a certain person."

"Who?"

"You."

"Me?" she said, feeling her cheeks flush.

He gazed at her steadily, his eyes not wavering. "Yes. I'm very interested in learning more about Melody Connelly."

CHAPTER 21

The heat on her cheeks wasn't just from the flickering fire. He wasn't asking because she was a famous Broadway singing star, or because he wanted to take advantage of her fame.

He was asking because he was interested in her as a person. As a fellow human being. And perhaps also because —

Stop, she told herself. *Don't go there.*

Over the past few years, she'd built barriers to protect herself — necessary safeguards to keep the clamoring world at bay. But now, up here in Heartsprings Valley, the need for those barriers seemed to be melting away.

"Darling," she said, "feel free. Ask away. After all, fair is fair."

"Well," he said, considering his words. "You mentioned your mom."

"Now safely at the Inn with Barbara, thank goodness."

"How about your dad? Tell me about him."

"I wish I could," Melody said, then paused. "He died when I was four."

"I'm sorry to hear that. What happened?"

She swallowed back a surge of emotion. "He was a long-haul truck driver, crossing a mountain pass in Colorado, when his truck went off the road into a ravine."

"Do you remember much about him?"

"Not nearly enough. Flashes of memory. I wish I remembered more."

"Tell me what you can."

It was an interesting question — she couldn't remember the last time someone had asked her that. She bit her lip for a moment, then said, "Little moments have stuck with me. He was so big and burly, like a mountain. He had a brown beard and a warm smile. He used to call me 'pumpkin.' He'd pick me up and hug me and whisper 'pumpkin' in my ear."

James smiled. "Sounds like you were close."

"I know I loved him very much."

"Any brothers or sisters?"

She shook her head. "Just me."

"Growing up without him — was that hard?"

"It was," she said, and paused. "You know, you're the first person in years to ask me — really ask me

— about my dad."

"I didn't mean to overstep."

"Oh, no — nothing of the sort. It's just…. I guess I'm curious why you asked."

"Why?" He considered her question. "Two reasons, I guess. One reason is, I want to get to know you."

Again, she felt a flush of pleasure.

He took a deep breath. "The second reason? How do I put this…?" His voice softened. "I guess the other reason is, I'm a dad with a daughter. Anna's grown up now, but it seems just yesterday she was a little girl, the same age as you were when…."

"When my dad died."

"I can't imagine not being in Anna's life. The thought of not being there for her…." He blinked back sudden emotion. "Losing your dad must have been really tough on you and your mom."

"It was," Melody said.

His brow furrowed. "Can I ask another question?"

"Sure."

"If I'm prying, tell me I'm prying. Seriously, tell me."

"Pry away."

He took a deep breath. "I'm sensing your mom is a bit of a sensitive subject."

Melody went still. *Was she really that obvious?* "You saying that because…?"

"You mentioned she was coming up, but you haven't really said much about her. Which got me to wondering. And then, a few minutes ago, when you talked about her being safe at the Inn, an expression passed over your face."

"An expression?"

"Not of sadness or frustration. But maybe a hint of those, mixed in with a helping of...."

She waited until he said:

"Hope."

"Hope?" she repeated.

He sat up straight. "Let me see if I can guess why you and your mom are here for Christmas." He gestured around the room. "Maybe even why you bought this big old house and fixed it up."

"You're going to guess."

"Right."

"About why my mom and I are here."

"Right."

"For Christmas."

"Right."

"Well, consider me intrigued."

She realized she'd tensed up. Not because he was asking — no, not because of that. Rather because, for reasons she didn't fully understand, she wanted him to be *right*.

He gave her a measured look. "I sense you and your mom have had your share of ups and downs. My gut is telling me you want to move past that. You want this Christmas to be a clean slate. A reset. A way to clear the decks and move forward without the baggage of the past weighing you down."

Melody inhaled as his words sank in. He'd used phrases she never would have — was "clear the decks" a sailing term? — but he wasn't wrong. In fact, he was spot-on. Which surprised her. This James fellow was more than just handy, helpful, and handsome. There was a depth to him, a quiet perceptiveness....

"I said too much, didn't I?" he said. "Sorry."

"Oh, no, no, no," Melody said. "Not at all. I'm just surprised — surprised that you saw all that."

"You sure I didn't overstep?"

"Not at all."

"I'm glad. I wouldn't want to make you upset."

"Has anyone ever told you you're a good noticer?"

He shrugged. "Not really."

"Somehow I doubt that."

"Well, maybe now and again."

They looked at each other as the fire glowed, the warmth from the flames reassuring her.

"I bet you notice a lot."

He shifted back onto his side, his eyes not leaving hers. "Sometimes."

"Tell me something you're noticing right now."

"Like what?"

"Something you wouldn't usually talk about."

He weighed her request for a few seconds, then said, "This might sound strange, but…."

"But what?"

"Nah. If I told you, I'd sound crazy."

"Try me. I'm good with crazy."

He took a deep breath, his gaze not leaving hers. "You're easy to talk with."

"Glad to hear that."

"You make me feel comfortable."

"I feel the same."

The fire's flickering flames seemed to be encouraging them, urging them to share their inner thoughts.

Her tone was soft. "Tell me."

He took another breath, then exhaled. "Sometimes, when I'm working on a piece of furniture, or fixing up a house, I'll feel its energy with me."

Her pulse quickened. "When you say 'energy,' what do you mean?"

"I mean a memory, sense, presence. It's hard to explain."

"A ghost?"

He shook his head. "Nothing that defined. More like a feeling or mood."

"I think I can relate," she said slowly. "Sometimes in New York, when I'm onstage in a grand old theater, I feel echoes of its history. Almost like the actors and audiences of years or even decades ago are still there, sharing the moment with me."

He nodded. "Like the echoes of the past aren't really in the past. Like they remain with us in the here and now."

"I've never thought of it like that."

"Neither have I," he confessed with a short laugh.

"Quiet waters run deep."

"They certainly do here."

"Here?"

"I feel an energy here," he said.

She blinked. "In this house?"

He nodded. "This proud old beauty has been through some rough times. But as soon as I laid eyes on it, I knew it was ready for a rebirth."

Her throat tightened. What he was saying — she'd experienced it as well. The second she'd seen this house, she'd felt its pull.

"Tell me about the energy here," she said.

"It's a good energy. A warm energy. A welcoming energy. I sense *gratitude*. It likes being fixed up again. It likes being lived in again. It's glad someone is here to call it home."

Tears threatened. *And tears wouldn't do.* She inhaled swiftly and blinked rapidly to keep them at bay.

"So the house approves?"

He chuckled. "It's humming a happy tune."

Relief flooded through her. "Does it know which wallpaper I should pick for the upstairs hallway?"

He cocked an ear and pretended to listen. "The one with the evergreen forest pattern."

She laughed. "No way the house just told you that."

"Oh, but it did," he said, a solemn expression on his face. Then he laughed. "Nah. I just like that wallpaper."

"I do, too."

He pointed to their empty mugs. "Ready for round two?"

She swung her legs off the sofa and stood up. "Round two, here we come."

CHAPTER 22

This time, their trip to the kitchen was smooth and perfectly choreographed. The earlier awkwardness was gone, replaced with an awareness, a sense about each other that hadn't been there before. They were in tune with each other. Without saying a word, they knew exactly what each of them would do next.

As she swirled the hot chocolate mix into her cup to speed up the dissolving, she realized she hadn't brought the flashlight — and that she didn't need it. Her kitchen was becoming familiar enough to navigate even in the near-darkness.

They brought their drinks back to the facing sofas and settled in.

Melody took a sip, the cocoa fortifying her for what she knew she was going to say next. Across from her on his couch, James seemed to understand she was working up to something. He remained silent, his expression thoughtful, waiting for her to speak.

"About my mom," she said.

He nodded, his gaze holding hers.

"I love her very much, but our relationship hasn't always been sweetness and light. In fact, for many years, there wasn't much of a relationship at all."

"Tell me why."

"You sure you want to hear all this?"

"Totally sure."

"You'll probably meet her."

"Are you going to tell me something that will cause me to not like her?"

"Oh, no, no, no. Nothing like that."

"So she's not a monster?"

"Oh, no."

"Or a nightmare?"

"No."

"Or a tyrant?"

A small smile appeared on her lips. "No."

"Does she act weird?"

She laughed. "No!"

"Then I'm good," he said. "I only have problems with weird-acting monster nightmare tyrants. If she's not one of those...."

"She's not any of those. There's not a mean bone in her body."

"Glad to hear that."

"She can be very generous and kind and giving."

"All of which sounds good."

"All of which *is* good," she said.

He didn't reply, instead allowing the silence to lengthen.

She sighed. "It's hard to explain."

"Give it a shot."

"Mom is ... insecure. She always has been. Her current husband is Husband Number Four."

His eyebrows rose. "Number Four?"

"His name is Benny. I like him. He's good for her. My issue isn't him."

"So your issue is...."

"She's never believed she can stand on her own two feet. She's always felt the need to be with someone. So when it comes to relationships, she's always rushed in. Way too fast, diving in deep before she even knows what the water's like."

"Ah."

"After my dad died, she was single for about a year before she met the guy who became Husband Number Two."

"What was he like?"

"I remember him being very nice, but he was older and not very active. He died of a heart attack a couple of years after they got married. I remember the funeral. I was seven."

"I'm sorry to hear that."

"It was after his death that my mom really started dating obsessively."

"That's a strong word."

"Well," she said, considering. "Unfortunately, I think it's accurate. She had a pattern. She'd meet someone and get excited. I'd help her get ready for her dates. For a while, it was fun. An adventure. Helping her get ready was a way for me to be part of her life. She was excited, so I was excited."

He nodded.

"But gradually, as I got older, I began to understand more. The relationships were ending in disappointment for her. She'd become sad and anxious."

"Which must have been tough on you."

"I was ten when Mom started dating the guy who would become Husband Number Three. I was at an age that I wanted — needed — her to focus on me. I was going through things and not doing too well in school and I needed her to be there."

"But she wasn't?"

She shook her head. "Not in the way I wanted. She was too busy doting on Gary — that was his name — and going on dates with him and leaving me with babysitters or my aunt. I felt neglected. I became angry and resentful."

He took a sip of his cocoa, giving her the space to continue.

She sighed. "When she told me she was marrying Gary, I got really mad." Tears threatened again, but with effort she managed to keep them at bay. "I felt betrayed."

"That must have been rough."

"It was Gary's third marriage as well. His first two had ended after he got caught cheating."

"Don't tell me — history repeated?"

"I was thirteen when I saw him kissing a woman at a local restaurant."

"Oh, geez."

"For three long days, I kept what I saw to myself. I tried to figure out what to say and who to say it to."

"What happened on the fourth day?"

"I confronted him."

James sat up. "You did *what*?"

She shrugged. "While my mom was in the kitchen getting dinner ready, I went to where he was sitting in the living room and told him what I'd seen."

James said, "What did he say?"

"He tried to deny it. I told him it was a waste of time to even bother trying."

"And then?"

"Mom overheard and asked what was going on."

"And then?"

"And then — it all came out."

"Wow."

She took a deep breath. Even now, more than two decades later, the memories of that painful night triggered an emotional response she found difficult to manage. "Mom moved us out — we were living in his house — and divorced him."

"You were thirteen?"

She nodded. "And very angry, unfortunately. Looking back, I see now how difficult it was for my mom. The cheating, the moving out, the divorce, dealing with me — all of that uncertainty and chaos and conflict."

"What was going on with you?"

She sighed. "A lot of it was just the usual growing pains. Typical teenage rebellion. But looking back, I know I was a handful. I've always pushed and pushed and pushed, even when I shouldn't."

He smiled. "I'm trying to picture you as a teen rebel."

"I dyed my hair black when I was fourteen."

His eyes widened. "You did *what*?"

"Black fingernail polish, black jewelry, black mascara, black clothes."

"What did your mom say?"

"She drew the line at tattoos."

"Man," he said, shaking his head. "I got lucky with Anna. Her big rebellion was studying too hard."

Melody laughed. "You got *very* lucky."

"How long did your goth phase last?"

"Until I got pulled into the high school drama club."

"Ah," he said. "Who pulled you in?"

"My theater teacher, Ms. Rhodes. She heard me

singing to myself in the hallway at school and asked
me to audition for a play."

"You'd never thought about performing before?"

"Not really. I was too caught up in my own
drama to understand what theater offered."

"Which was?"

"Escape. Pure, simple, blissful escape. Despite my
nerves and reluctance, I let Ms. Rhodes persuade me
to audition. When I got up on that stage and opened
my mouth, I realized I'd discovered something
magical."

"Did you get the part?"

"Of course!" she said with a playful grin. "And
had the time of my life."

"You found your tribe."

"Exactly." She was pleased he'd put it that way —
she used the same language herself. "My tribe of
creative, talented misfits."

"Are they still your tribe?"

"Now and forever. I can't imagine the theater not
being part of my life."

"So … how does Heartsprings Valley fit in?"

The question came casually, but Melody got the
sense her answer mattered to him.

And mattered to her, too.

She took a deep breath. "I'm here to figure that
out." She took a sip of cocoa, its warmth reassuring
her. "I came up here on a lark two years ago, after a
breakup. I knew nothing about Heartsprings Valley.

But from the moment I arrived, this little town grabbed me in a way I haven't been grabbed since that first audition back in high school."

He liked hearing that, she could tell. And she knew why. She recognized what was going on here. His interest in her was clear.

And hers in him?

She swallowed back a jolt of excitement. She needed to move this conversation to safer ground — *pronto*.

"So," she said, "are you from here?"

He nodded. "Born and raised. Lived here my entire life."

"Was that always the plan?"

"When I was younger, I thought about moving away. I've always wanted to give city living a try. But then we had Anna, and…."

"You stayed."

Another nod. "Heartsprings Valley is home. It's where our family and friends are. And with Anna doing so well at school and being such a great kid, there was never any question about upending that and moving away."

"After the divorce, did she live with her mom?"

He nodded. "She lived with Tammy through ninth grade. When Tammy married Ed and moved across the lake to Eagle Cove, Anna decided she wanted to stay in school in Heartsprings Valley, so she moved in with me."

"Because of her friends?"

"And her teachers."

"Ah, yes, the future scholar."

He smiled. "Now that she's in Boston for college, I don't have the same reason for staying. I'm open to giving a new place a shot. But what can I say? I like it here."

"Your friends, your family…."

"My parents live here, and my brother and his family."

"What about your … girlfriend?"

She'd asked it as casually as she could. As neutrally as she could. She willed her face to appear interested in what she hoped was a casually neutral way.

He blinked. "I'm not dating anyone right now."

"Oh, I see," she said, pleased that her tone remained level.

Beneath his beard, did his cheeks flush? "Anna's on a mission to change that. She says I need to get out there and mix it up and join the dating scene. She says her dad's too young to be some old fuddy-duddy."

"Her word, fuddy-duddy?" Melody asked with a smile.

"My daughter has a very extensive vocabulary," he said dryly.

"Is she right?"

"Sure. But one of the downsides of a small town is...."

"A limited dating pool."

He shrugged. "The way I see it, either you hit it off with someone or you don't."

"When you know, you know."

"Pretty much right away."

His gaze intensified. Suddenly, the room felt very warm. The fireplace was throwing off heat like crazy.

Melody swallowed, irritated by the flood of emotion surging through her. She was a grown woman. From time to time she met attractive men, and from time to time they expressed interest in her.

Which meant she knew how to deal with situations like the one she found herself in now.

So why did she suddenly feel like an inexperienced teenager?

"I went to your website," she said, the words coming out of her mouth before she could stop them.

"My furniture site?" he replied, his brow furrowing, clearly wondering why she'd jumped to a completely different topic.

"The site has wonderful photography," she said, the words again leaving without warning. "Who did the photos?"

"Anna. The site was her idea."

Melody nodded. This daughter of his was growing more impressive by the second. "How long have you had the site?"

"She did it the summer before she went to college, so ... a year-and-a-half?"

"Have you generated any business from it?"

He nodded. "Actually, yes. Several commissions."

"You sound surprised."

"I was. I am. I guess I didn't think that kind of marketing stuff mattered."

"It only matters if it aligns with your aims."

She paused as she realized: *I'm channeling Nigel.*

James was staring at her like he'd just been introduced to a new side of her. He'd met the Broadway star, the new homeowner, and the girl with the complicated childhood. Now he was meeting the media-savvy professional who knew a thing or two about promotion and marketing.

"I bet there are things I can improve on the site," he said.

"I did have a couple of thoughts."

"Lay 'em on me."'

"You should add your photo to your bio," she said right away.

He blinked, surprised. "Why's that?"

Because handsome sells, she almost blurted out.

Instead she said, "Because people are curious. They want to know more about the artist."

To her surprise, she saw him tense at the word *artist.*

She sat up, puzzled. *Could it be...?*

"James," she said slowly, "you do know you're an artist, don't you?"

His mouth opened, then closed.

"I...."

"Oh, no, no, no, darling," Melody said, sitting up straighter, her senses on full alert. "Don't you dare."

"I've never really thought of myself as...."

"Stop," Melody said. "Don't you dare utter those words."

He blinked again. "What words?"

"The words denying who you are."

"I don't mean...."

"James, I mean it."

"Well, it's just that...."

"It's just what?"

"Well, I've only just started."

Melody frowned. This simply would not do. "Let me ask you some questions."

"Okay."

He was wary, she realized. His guard was up. Which was confusing. Why this response from him? Then suddenly she saw, with a flash of insight:

He's ready for his next chapter, but he doesn't know he's ready.

Maybe, if she approached this right, she could help him lay the foundation.

"When you have free time, do you often find yourself in your woodworking studio, working on projects?"

"Yes," he said.

"Do you love doing those projects?"

"Yes."

"When you're doing those projects, do you feel completely immersed in them?"

"Yes."

"Do you study what other furniture makers and woodworkers have done?"

"Yes."

"Are you constantly striving to improve your craft?"

"Yes."

"Do you put your heart and soul into what you do?"

"Yes."

"Is it satisfying to share your craft with others?"

"Yes."

She gave him a reassuring smile. "Then that means only one thing."

"It means...."

"It means you're an artist."

This time, he didn't object. He kept his mouth shut as he chewed on her words. "It's been a side hobby for a while."

She nodded. "A passion."

"I've always been drawn to woodworking and furniture design, but...."

"You needed to pay the bills."

"Right."

"So you worked in construction."

"Right."

"And did the furniture crafting on the side."

"Right."

"Until your life began to change in the last year or two."

He looked at her, his wariness returning. "What do you mean?"

"One big change: Your little girl grew up and became a young woman and moved away."

He blinked rapidly, as if battling back tears.

"Another big change: You're beginning to connect with the audience for your work. The commissions you've received, the custom pieces you've done, are nudges from the universe."

He raised an eyebrow. "The universe?"

"Shorthand, darling. Just my feeble attempt to wrap words around the vast, unfathomable nature of life's eternal grandeur."

"And the nudges?"

"Oh, that's easier. The nudges are the universe telling you it's time to broaden and deepen your commitment to your craft."

He smiled at her, appreciation in his eyes. "You're kind of a revelation."

She blinked, pleased. "I am?"

"Your way of thinking is eye-opening."

"I've been pursuing my craft for a long time."

"I bet you could show me a lot."

"Always happy to help a fellow artist."

He chuckled. "Artist," he repeated, as if testing the word.

"Am I right?" she asked.

He took a deep breath. "Sure."

"Not good enough. I want you to hear your passion." She raised her voice. "Are you an artist?"

"Yes."

"Louder."

"Yes!"

"What are you?"

"An artist!" he almost yelled.

"Hurrah!" she said, sitting up to applaud him. "Bravo, darling, bravo!"

They both laughed, pleased and self-conscious.

At that moment, Buster chose to join them. He sidled up to James and rubbed himself along his sofa, shooting Melody a look that seemed to say, *What's up with all this yelling, you noisy humans?*

"I wonder where he's been," Melody said.

"Up to no good, no doubt," James said as he reached down to stroke his fur.

Buster leaned into James's hand, purring loudly.

"This is how he is most of the time," James said. "Friendly as all get-out."

"He enjoys hanging out?"

"He loves it."

Buster turned toward Melody and strolled over to her. With a grace that impressed her, especially with that awkward cone around his neck, he leaped onto her couch and onto her. He stared at her a long moment, then settled down on top of her blanket-covered stomach and began purring loudly.

"You are such a darling," she said softly, reaching out to run her hand over his soft fur.

Buster closed his eyes and purred louder, pressing himself into her hand.

"See?" James said. "Told you he likes you."

"And I him. He's adorable."

She threw a grin at James, who grinned back, his lively grey eyes radiating appreciation and interest. Clearly, when it came to *her*, James Newcastle wasn't shy at all.

She knew then that she was going to have to ask herself her big questions again:

At this moment in my life, what matters most?

What do I want to commit myself to, fully and without reservation?

Because without warning, the answers she'd given herself that very afternoon seemed — how to put it?

Shockingly incomplete.

CHAPTER 23

Melody cracked her eyelids open, emerging reluctantly from the blessed comforts of sleep. She shifted onto her side and felt the soft towel-pillow caress her cheek. Beneath her crinkly tarp-blanket, every inch of her felt safe and warm.

Natural light was filling the room through the floor-to-ceiling windows. Which meant it was dawn, or just past. She stretched her back and shoulders slowly, pleased to not sense any discomfort. Much to her surprise, her makeshift sleeping arrangements had proved quite restful.

She turned her gaze to the other couch and found it empty. She hadn't heard James get up. She listened closely for a moment, but didn't hear any sounds indicating where he might be in the house.

She needed caffeine. In the worst way.

Alas, 'twas not to be. Because she had no coffee. Or tea. Or even a kettle.

Urgh.

The previous evening almost seemed like a dream. A night of discovery and surprise. She and James had talked late into the night in front of the flickering fire, munching on scones and candy bars and popcorn, telling each other stories from their childhoods, their jobs, their dating histories — everything that had come to mind. She hadn't held back and neither, she sensed, had he.

Now a new day had dawned. With a soft groan, she reached out and groped for her phone on the floor next to the couch, then turned it on and checked for cell service. Still no signal.

It was time to deal with reality. Starting with: Where had James gone? She untangled herself from her tarp-blanket and swung her legs off the couch, then stood and stretched.

She made her way into the kitchen, rubbing the sleep from her eyes and running her hands through her hair. At the sink, she let the hot water run, then splashed water over her face.

A hot shower would be nice. Then she remembered:

She had no body wash. Or soap. Or shampoo.

Urgh.

From now on, she *really* needed a list!

Through the kitchen window in front of her farmhouse sink, the morning light was getting brighter. Fresh snow glistened on the ground.

Movement outside at the far end of the meadow caught her eye. It was James, leaving the woods and walking back toward the house. He looked very much at home up here, his steps sure and confident. When he reached the SUVs, he did a walk-around, looking for damage, then made his way up the porch steps.

A few seconds later, she heard the sound of the front door opening.

"In here!" she said, loudly enough for him to hear.

He pushed open the kitchen door a moment later, a grin on his face. "Hey, you."

"Didn't hear you get up."

"Didn't want to wake you."

"Saw you coming back. What's the verdict?"

"Two big branches blocking the way out. I managed to pull one to the side. But the other one…."

"The one we tried to move last night?"

He nodded. "We'll need help. They'll be up later to clear it."

"How much ice did we get?"

"A lot," he sighed. "But if it warms up enough today — and it feels like it could — most of it will melt."

"I don't suppose you have any phone service."

He shook his head. "Not yet."

"And no electricity?"

He turned to the light switch and flipped it on. Nothing. "Nope."

"I just realized what I want to do."

"What's that?" he said, curiosity in his tone.

"Check out my new dining room. And my new dining table."

He swallowed, a flush rising on his cheeks, but didn't object. "After you," he said, gesturing for her to lead.

She made her way to the back of the kitchen, through a swinging door she hadn't passed through yet, then through her butler's pantry — more lovely storage! — into her dining room.

Across the lake, the morning sun had broken through the clouds and was bathing the room in light. The room was wonderfully proportioned — long enough for a big table, wide enough for sideboards along the walls, with big windows offering a view of the valley below. Intricate wood paneling, now fully restored, gleamed in the morning light.

But all those details receded as she beheld the dining table that held the place of honor in the center of the room.

Her breath caught. It was *gorgeous*. The table was built to seat eight, with add-on leaves available for the ends to expand seating to twelve. Made with reclaimed cedar and stained a rich golden brown, the wood complemented the paneling on the walls, yet retained a distinctive quality all its own.

"James," she breathed, "the table is beautiful."

"Thank you," he said quietly.

She approached it, her hand drawn irresistibly to the table's live edge. There was a flow here that seemed so effortless. She ran her fingers over it, enjoying the curves and dips, delighting at formerly rough spots smoothed over ever-so-slightly.

A feeling of connection rushed through her. This was a table built to be a gathering place for family and friends — beautiful enough to impress, solid enough to bear the weight of bountiful meals, resilient and forgiving enough to handle the inevitable bumps and dents and dings.

And interesting enough to always surprise.

Yes, that was its extra ingredient, the spark that made it special. This table's appeal, its essence, lay in its ability to reveal itself gradually.

No matter how closely she studied it, there would always be something new to discover. A new line, a new curve, a new swirl in the wood, a new depth of color awaiting her when she looked at it in a new light or from a new angle.

She flash-forwarded to how the room would soon look with carpeting on the floor, sideboards against the walls, curtains framing the large windows, chairs pulled up around the table, and a restored chandelier lighting the room.

Even when joined by those other beautiful pieces, her new dining table would be the star.

All due to the man — the artist — now standing by her side.

"Thank you, James," she said, her throat tight with unexpected emotion. "I can't tell you how happy I am to have your beautiful table in my new home."

She looked up at him and found his grey eyes shining with emotion. "It means a lot to hear you say that."

She knew it then: Last night hadn't been a fluke. What she'd felt then — she felt it even more now.

James was feeling it, too, she knew. His gaze was fixed on her, his grey eyes alive with interest. She found herself leaning closer to him, and sensed him leaning toward her —

Until a sound from somewhere outside yanked her out of the moment. It was the roar of a machine — an engine. James heard it, too, his shoulders tensing, his brow furrowing.

The sound was getting louder by the second.

"What in the world?" she said.

"No clue."

Without waiting another second, they rushed to the front door, which James opened and —

Melody gasped. The sound was so loud now!

And then —

A helicopter appeared!

Slowly, it lowered itself over the center of her open meadow, its blades scattering snow and ice, whipping forth a wind that reached her and James with enough force to push them back.

Hands over her eyes, she watched the chopper touch down.

A figure jumped out. A man.

He ducked down and ran toward them.

Melody gasped again as she realized who it was.

Derek!

CHAPTER 24

She could only stare, shocked and overwhelmed, as Derek dashed up to them like the action star he was.

What in the world was going on?

"Melody!" he said.

For a long moment, her mouth didn't work. Finally, she managed to say, "Derek, what are you doing here?"

"I came to rescue you," he said, pulling her in for a hug.

Rescue me?

"Derek, I —"

Her cheek was pressed against his coat, his arms holding her tight. "And reunite you with your mom."

She blinked with surprise. "My mom?" she said, disengaging from him. "Is everything okay?"

"She's fine — safe and sound at the Inn — and eager to see you."

Derek looked so determined standing there — just like he did on-screen. Every inch the rescuing hero. The helicopter started powering down, its blades slowing, the deafening roar fading.

With a blinding rush, the dots began connecting.

The previous night on the phone, Barbara had mentioned a surprise.

The surprise must have been Derek's sudden arrival at the Inn.

And at the Inn, he must have met her mom.

But —

"The helicopter?" she said, gesturing behind him.

"Rented this morning."

"And you want me to…?"

"Come with."

Come with? "In *that*?"

"Yes."

"Right now?"

For the first time since he dashed up, uncertainty flashed across his face. Until now, everything had gone according to script. His dramatic arrival, her surprise and shock, her inability to speak. But she could see him wonder: Why was the heroine hesitating? Why wasn't she rushing back into his arms, filled with gratitude, tears of joy flowing?

Why didn't the heroine want to be rescued?

"Derek," she said, "let me introduce you to James."

Derek blinked and frowned, then turned toward James as if suddenly realizing he was there.

For a long second, the two men took stock of each other. Neither was happy about the other's presence, she immediately sensed. Both, in their own ways, were take-charge guys who preferred to live life on their own terms. They even looked similar — similar ages and builds, James an inch taller and Derek clean-shaven, but otherwise cut from the same cloth.

Both had very subtly tensed up, like they instinctively understood the threat they posed to each other.

James stuck out his hand. "James Newcastle. Pleased to meet you."

Derek took the hand in his. "Derek Davies. Pleasure's mine."

Before the handshake became awkward, Melody jumped in.

"James is a furniture designer and wood craftsman working on the house."

"Barbara mentioned you weren't stuck up here alone."

"Thank goodness, no. I don't know what I would have done without James."

Derek turned back to James. "Glad you were here to help out."

James shrugged. "Glad I was able to."

"There's room for both of you in the chopper."

"I'm pretty sure the roads will be cleared in a bit," James said, then started suddenly. "Hang on, my phone vibrated." He pulled it out of his pocket and looked at it. "Service is back."

"Oh, thank goodness," Melody said.

"A bunch of texts," he said, scanning the screen, "including one from Clara. Help's on the way, sometime before noon."

"Hurray!"

James swung his attention back to Derek. "I appreciate the offer for the ride, but I'll stick around here and help clear the branch."

"If you're sure," Derek said.

"I'm good." He turned to Melody. "You should go. I'm sure your mom can't wait to see you."

"But my car…."

"You'll be able to get it when you come up later."

He was right, of course. Someone could drive her up. Still….

"Besides," he added, "how often do you get to see Heartsprings Valley from the air?"

"Are you sure?"

"The view is spectacular."

Melody looked up at him, so serious and determined. He really did want what was right for her. Even if it meant their ice-bound adventure was coming to an end.

She turned to Derek. "I'll get my things."

He nodded. "I'll tell the pilot to get ready."

She left the two men on the porch and stepped back inside, closing the door behind her, unsettled and jumpy and frazzled.

Stuff. She needed her *stuff.* She returned to her couch and grabbed her winter coat and gloves. What else? Her phone. And her handbag.

Was she missing anything?

She returned to the front door and nearly opened it when she realized:

Her boots!

She returned to the fireplace, grabbed her now-dry boots, and sat down to slip them on. She really should help clean up, she realized, taking in the candy wrappers and popcorn container on the floor between their couches. It wouldn't be right to leave their campsite in its current state.

She heard the front door open and close again, the roar of the helicopter briefly filling the room.

James appeared. "So," he said slowly. "That's Derek Davies."

"The one and only," she said as she started to fold her tarp blanket.

"The guy you were dating two years ago."

"The very one."

"You seemed surprised to see him."

"Stunned," she said, turning to her towel. "And not just because of the helicopter."

He paused, as if unsure what to say. Then, as if making a decision, he squared his shoulders and said, "Melody, I would like to ask you out on a date."

She went still, pleasure jolting through her. "You would?"

"Yes. A real date."

He looked so handsome standing there, the hints of salt-and-pepper in his dark brown hair now visible in the morning light. He seemed so serious. So purposeful. So hopeful.

It was odd to think of going on a first date with him. The normal order of things was out of kilter. First dates were usually about two people beginning to get to know each other.

She and James had already done that. The previous night had been the equivalent of four or five dates — maybe more.

It would be so simple to say yes.

All she had to do was open her mouth and let the word roll off her tongue.

Say yes! her heart said eagerly.

And yet she found herself hesitating, pulling back.

Was James part of her next chapter? Her fresh start?

If so, what was Derek doing here?

What was the universe trying to tell her?

"James," she said.

"Yes?" he said, the first hint of anxiety crossing his face. She could see him starting to second-guess himself, wondering: Had he moved too fast? Had he misread her? Had he misjudged what they'd shared the previous night? Was this Derek guy the one she really wanted?

"I would love to," she said.

"Good," he said, clearly relieved.

"We'll have to figure out the when and where, what with the holidays and finishing up the house and my mom here and —"

He nodded. "Totally get it." He glanced at their campsite. "I'll handle cleanup. You need to get going."

"Are you sure?"

"Absolutely."

She found herself not moving. "And you?"

"Once the road is clear, I'll head home to check on Anna, then come back this afternoon to keep working. I assume that's okay?"

"Yes, of course. I'll be in and out as well, either here or down at the Inn with my mom...."

They looked at each other, as if unwilling to part. They'd spent an evening and a morning side by side — and Melody suddenly understood, with a clarity so sharp it was almost painful, that she didn't want their time together to end.

"I'm sure your mom can't wait to see you," he said. "I look forward to meeting her."

"I can't wait to introduce the two of you."

She set the folded towel on the couch, then picked

up her handbag. She found herself swallowing back a rush of emotion. Should she hug him goodbye? Shake his hand?

"Thank you," she said. "For everything."

"No need to thank me," he said, his eyes not leaving her, alert to her every move. "I wouldn't trade last night for anything."

A hug. Yes, at least a hug. She found herself stepping toward him. As one, their arms went around each other, James pulling her in close.

"See you soon," she whispered, her cheek pressed against his chest.

She took a deep breath, then forced herself to step back and place a smile on her face.

Determined to not look back, she turned and walked out the door.

CHAPTER 25

That evening, after a whirlwind day of nonstop activity, Melody finally lay her head on her downy pillow on her lovely bed in her beloved Harvest Room in the beautiful Heartsprings Valley Inn and allowed herself to relax.

How to describe the day she'd just had?

Disjointed? Yes, most certainly. Along with —

Unsettling.

But also vivid. And memorable.

A good day, with so much worth celebrating, even if she had no idea what the various pieces all meant. There were so many individual moments and sensations to sort through and digest.

She let herself rewind the day, trying not to pause or analyze as she replayed the rush of events.

Starting with that morning in the dining room

with James — the moment in which they had nearly kissed. Everything had felt so right....

Don't dwell, she reminded herself. *At least not yet. Let the day play out.*

Then the interruption — Derek's shocking arrival — throwing everything into confusion. Despite their history, her former beau clearly retained the ability to tug at her feelings. What he'd done — the trouble he'd gone to — was touching. Unnecessary, but touching. Was it all right to be simultaneously grateful to him, and annoyed at his timing?

Honestly, how did she feel about him coming up here, anyway?

Don't dwell, she told herself again.

Then the bone-rattling helicopter ride — the disorienting rush of lifting into the air, the roar of the engine and clatter of the blades nearly overwhelming her, the vibrations reaching deep inside and shaking her to her core, with only earphones and a seat belt strapped snug across her chest to protect her.

How lovely her new house had looked from above.

And how her heart had lurched at the sight of James staring up at her, watching her go.

And then Derek, at that very instant, reaching out and taking her hand in his. "I'm so glad you're safe, Melody," he'd said, his voice thick with emotion, his movie-star charisma impossible to ignore.

Oh, what to think about the waves of gratitude and longing coursing through her?

Gratitude toward Derek, certainly. And of course toward James, who had been there for her in every way.

But longing for whom?

And then the helicopter swooping over the valley, the lake shining like a jewel in the morning sun, her adopted town sparkling under a blanket of ice and snow, its beauty bringing tears to her eyes.

Then settling over the high school's football field at the outskirts of town, right at the fifty-yard line, trembling at the sight of her mom and Benny at the sidelines, bundled up against the cold, awaiting her arrival.

Then Derek saying, as the helicopter touched down, "Your mom and Benny will take you to the Inn."

It was funny how, the instant the helicopter returned to solid ground, her sense of time had returned to a more normal flow.

She'd turned to Derek, confused. "You're not coming?"

He gestured to the pilot. "We've been asked to help with search-and-rescue — to check on remote roads that may be blocked."

"It's great you can pitch in to help."

He was pleased about being asked, she could tell. Being part of a storm recovery effort fit into his action-star persona. "If I'm in a position to be of assistance...."

She took a deep breath. "Derek, thank you for...." She paused, not sure what to say next. Somehow, *rescue* didn't seem like the right way to describe what had just happened. "Thank you for coming to get me."

He aimed his megawatt grin at her. "This feels like the right time to ask. How about that coffee date?"

She swallowed. She'd been expecting the question. And knew that the only answer was —

"Of course."

"Tomorrow?"

"Tomorrow's fine."

He pushed open the helicopter door and hopped out, then extended his hand. She took off her headphones and unfastened her seat belt. With his help, she eased back onto solid ground.

"Thank you again!" she yelled over the roar.

"See you at the Inn!" he yelled back.

As he hopped back into the chopper, she dashed across the icy field, head bent low, the wind whipping through her hair.

Straight into the wide-open arms of her mother. Oh, how good it felt to wrap her arms around her!

Her mom hugged her tight. "Darling, you made it!"

"Mom, so good to see you!"

Together, they watched the helicopter lift off the ground and fly away. Benny pulled them both in for hug, shielding them from some of the helicopter's force.

"You had us worried last night," he said.

"I'm so glad you're both here," Melody replied.

As the helicopter's roar faded, Melody pulled back from the hug to inspect her mom. Yes, her mom looked good — happy and relieved, her usual anxieties temporarily at bay. She'd turned sixty earlier that year. Though not as tall as Melody, the two of them had the same coloring — clear pale skin, flaming red hair, striking green eyes. When they were together, there was never any doubt they were mother and daughter. As usual during the cold winter months, her mom was dressed as if preparing for an Arctic expedition — cap on head, scarf around her neck, mittens on hands, a huge winter coat that ran nearly to her knees, with winter boots protecting her feet.

Standing next to her, Benny was like a well-dressed bodyguard — tall and wide and snappily dressed in a gray wool overcoat, slacks, and dress shoes, a burgundy scarf around his neck. With a full head of gray hair that he kept carefully coiffed and an expressive face with prominent eyes and nose and jowls, he came across as comfortably old-school. He knew his style and enjoyed living it. Beneath his long overcoat, she had no doubt he was dressed, as always, in a blazer and dress shirt.

From the instant she'd met him, she'd liked him, and not just because of his fondness for a good whisky and a good story. No, what had truly won her over was his protectiveness toward her mom. He was unfailingly attentive and thoughtful, and it was clear that her comfort and happiness were his top priorities.

"It's cold out here," he said. "Let's get you back to the Inn."

On the way, Melody gave them a highlight reel of the previous day and night.

"I'm glad this James fellow was there," her mom said.

"Me, too," Melody replied.

"How old is he again?"

Melody pursed her lips, aware of what her mom really wanted to know. Had something in her tone of voice alerted her mom to what was swirling through her head? "You'll probably meet him later, at the house," she said, sidestepping the question. "After I get cleaned up, I'd love to take you up and give you a full tour."

"That sounds wonderful."

The instant they arrived at the Inn, Barbara swept Melody into the kitchen, where a breakfast of scrambled eggs, bacon, toast and — yes! — coffee awaited.

Skillfully, with her mom and Benny at hand,

Barbara proceeded to extract every detail about her snowbound night.

"You had *popcorn* for dinner?" Barbara repeated, horrified.

"And hot chocolate," Melody said.

Barbara's eyes narrowed. "What kind of hot chocolate?"

"Instant," Melody confessed. "I bought it at the gas station."

Barbara shuddered. "I need to make you more eggs."

"No, I'm fine," Melody insisted. "It was fun, actually. James and I pretended we were camping. We set up a little campsite next to the fire."

"Ah, yes, James." Barbara glanced briefly at her mom. "So you two got along?"

"We did. He couldn't have been more helpful. Or better company."

"What did you all talk about?"

"Oh, lots of stuff. His woodworking, his daughter Anna, other things...." The thought came then: They had a reason for asking. An agenda was at play. A flush rose in her cheeks.

Barbara said, "Well, let me tell you, when you told me he was up there with you, I felt so relieved. I've always liked him." She turned to Melody's mom. "He's very handsome, by the way."

"Oh, is he?" her mom replied, far too innocently.

Melody shook her head, her suspicions

confirmed. "Listen, you two, that's not gonna fly. No way, no how. I know what you're up to."

"Up to, dear?" Barbara said, also far too innocently.

"You're indulging in Heartsprings Valley's favorite pastime."

"What's that?" her mom asked.

"Meddling."

Barbara laughed. "Oh, come now. Last night, while you and James were camping up at your new house, your mom and I had a chance to talk. It was perfectly natural for us to talk about James and what a good man he is."

Her mom reached out to Melody and gave her hand a squeeze. "I'm glad the two of you had fun. It's a good sign."

Melody sighed, refusing to take the *it's-a-good-sign* bait. "Mom…."

Her mom sat back in her seat. "Message received, darling. We'll back off. Though I do need to ask about yesterday's other surprise."

Barbara chimed in. "Talk about a surprise. Biggest shock of my life!"

Melody tensed. Indeed, what was she going to say about Derek? What could she say, with her insides roiling with confusion and uncertainty?

"Darling," her mom said, turning serious, "is Derek back in the picture?"

Melody took a deep breath. "No, he's not. At

least, not in the way you might think." Briefly, she told them about their encounter in New York. "In the helicopter, he asked me out for coffee. After all the trouble he went to, the least I could do was say yes."

She almost added: *Though I also have a coffee date with James.*

But instead she found herself holding back.

Which brought forth a question:

Why?

Maybe because she didn't want to reward their blatant attempt at meddling?

Or maybe because the spark, the connection, with James was so new and fresh that she wasn't quite ready to share anything yet?

Or maybe because Derek's appearance had thrown her into such a state of tumult that she needed to figure out what in the world she really, truly wanted before allowing any words to leave her mouth?

She turned to Barbara. "Do you have a piece of paper and a pen I can use?"

"Of course," Barbara said. She got up, opened a drawer near the kitchen door, found what Melody was looking for, and handed them to her.

"If there's one thing last night taught me," Melody said, "it's that I need to start writing down lists."

"Ah," Barbara said.

"No more forgetting important things. I'm a homeowner now. It's time to up my game."

Her mom smiled. "Benny and I are happy to help."

"Perfect," Melody said, twirling the pen in her hand. "Then let's get started!"

CHAPTER 26

*A*nd get started they did. List in hand, Melody and her mom and Benny tore through the rest of the day. After Melody dashed upstairs for a much-needed shower and change of clothes, the three of them shopped up a storm, hitting store after store along the town's main square.

With bags of goods loaded into Benny's SUV, they headed up to her new home on Summit Lane. As promised, the roads had been cleared, and much of the ice had already melted away.

When they reached the house, they found James and Luke already there. After Melody introduced everyone, the men helped bring their purchases inside.

As she watched James set her new coffee-maker on the kitchen counter, she felt the same jolt of pleasure at seeing him again.

She felt an urge to pull him aside for a private moment. But with her mom, Benny, and Luke awaiting her next move, she immediately realized that a private conversation was probably not going to happen.

"James," she asked, "did Anna get through the storm okay?"

"Oh, sure, she was totally fine." He swung toward her with a grin. "Though I got barraged with questions when I got home, most of them about you."

Melody didn't miss the way her mom hid a smile while watching and listening to the two of them. "Well, I look forward to getting to know her better."

"She's looking forward to that, too." He turned to her mom. "And how was your morning?"

"Busy!" her mom said. "We've been going nonstop since we picked up Melody at the high school."

"And where's Derek?"

He asked the question in a neutral, casual way. But she noticed his shoulders tense slightly as he waited for an answer.

Melody jumped in. "Derek and the helicopter pilot are helping with search-and-rescue. We'll see him later at the Inn."

There was more that James wanted to ask her, and more he wanted to say to her, she sensed. So before the moment could become awkward, Melody announced it was time to give her mom and Benny a house tour.

"We'll be downstairs," Luke said.

"See you in a bit," Melody replied, then ushered her mom and Benny away.

After a brisk but thorough walk-through of each floor, accompanied by the appropriate amount of *ooh*ing and *aah*ing, the three of them made their way down to the media room, where James and Luke were working on trim.

"One thing, Melody," Luke said. "We've rescheduled move-in day for the day after tomorrow. That okay?"

"Of course. But are you sure? Do you really think everything in town will be back to normal by then?"

"It should be," he said, then glanced at his watch. "Speaking of, we should pack up and head out. Temperatures will drop tonight. The roads will get icy again."

After the previous night's storm, no one needed convincing. Melody said, "Benny, I'll drive down in my SUV, and you can follow me in yours, okay?"

Benny nodded, and he and her mom headed up the stairs.

Melody turned to James. "Thank you again for everything last night."

His gaze didn't waver. "It was great meeting your mom and Benny."

"You heading out soon?"

He nodded. "In a few. And I'll be back tomorrow — still a lot to do."

"Thank you. Then I guess I'll … see you soon?"

"Count on it."

She felt the same pull again — the same impulse to hug him, or even more, to — *no, no, no, now was not the time.*

Instead, she arranged a bright smile on her face and said to him and Luke, very briskly, "See you soon!"

On the drive back to the Inn, momentarily alone in her SUV, she found her attention being pulled again toward what increasingly felt like a dilemma. Forcefully, she pushed the thought away. Today was *not* the day to delve into emotional uncertainty. The last thing she needed now was that kind of distraction. Because nothing mattered more than creating the perfect Christmas for her mom.

It felt good to remember that, she realized. The clarity was calming.

And now to turn her clarity into a reality…. Her hand reached for the dial on the radio. Turning the volume way up, she sang along to the music, focusing with determination on the lyrics, trying to get each word exactly right, occasionally glancing behind to make sure Benny and her mom were following.

Back at the Inn, she pushed forward with the same *lose-yourself-in-the-moment* technique by bustling with her mom into the kitchen to help Barbara make dinner. Benny and Stu joined them, whiskies in hand, as things got closer to being done. When Derek arrived after a day in the helicopter, the room really got hopping.

Soon enough, everyone was pitching in and the kitchen seemed to overflow with conversation and laughter. One thing she'd always admired about Derek was how good he was at putting people at ease. With Barbara's cheerful banter and Benny's natural gregariousness thrown into the mix, Melody was relieved to find the flow of discussion moving lightly and enjoyably from topic to topic. When Barbara's chicken cacciatore casserole emerged piping hot from the oven, they moved to the dinner table and dug in.

Derek really was very charming, Melody admitted. Not only were Barbara and Stu sold, but she could tell that her mom and Benny were warming up as well. He was full of good stories, he was a good listener, and he was considerate. Beneath that handsome exterior beat the heart of a decent, caring person. She'd seen the same qualities in him while they were dating. It was these qualities that had led her to open herself to a dream of a future with him.

The lovely food and enjoyable banter were so relaxing, the warm glow from the chandelier above so warm and glowing, the fullness of her stomach after enjoying Barbara's delicious dinner so reassuring. For a moment, the previous night seemed like a faraway dream. But then, without warning, she found herself recalling the tender way James had gazed at her in front of the fire — and the tug she'd felt as she'd leaned in toward him for the kiss-that-almost-was.

Was Derek's arrival a message from the universe? Or was the ice storm the message?

What was the universe trying to tell her?

She felt it then — a wave of overwhelming tiredness that had been patiently biding its time all day, hovering on the outskirts of her awareness, finally stepping up and clearing its throat and saying, *Girl, it's time to get thee to bed.*

She set down her glass of wine and waited for the conversation to come to a natural lull, then said, "Everyone, I'm afraid I'm going to have to head up to bed. I'm bushed."

"Well, I'm amazed you made it this long," Barbara said. "After the night and day you had."

"If you'd like, I can help clean up...."

"No need, dear. We've got it covered. You get upstairs."

Melody gave her a grateful nod and rose from her chair. "I'm so glad to be here with all of you," she said, her gaze moving to each of them, including Derek. "Thank you for everything you did to make this such a memorable day."

CHAPTER 27

*T*he next morning, Melody awoke to the familiar sound of her phone vibrating on her bedside table. She cracked an eye open and did her best to glare the phone into silence — a technique that never worked, despite her best efforts — before giving up and reaching out from the lovely warmth of her comforter and bringing the phone to her face and turning it on and —

Oh, my.

She bolted upright with surprise.

Text messages were flying, one after another — most of them from friends in New York.

"Are you okay?"

"OMG — so glad you survived!"

"How are you holding up? Anything you need, let us know!"

There were dozens of texts, urgent and rushed

and even frantic, all of them assuming that she'd just been through some sort of horrible life-and-death experience.

What in the world?

It was three minutes after eight, according to her phone. The light coming in through the windows was bright and sunny. She'd slept deeply and dreamlessly. Her bed was cozy and soft and really just plain wonderful.

But somehow, her friends thought she was in trouble?

Still struggling to become fully awake, she blinked as a call came in.

Nigel?

She picked up. "Darling, how are you?"

"My dear," Nigel said, his crisp English accent a bracing tonic to her ears, his voice carrying effortlessly across thousands of miles in the blink of an eye. "That is my question for you." There was an edge in his tone — a tone she'd heard before, one that meant he was restraining himself, doing his best *not* to give vent to his true feelings. "How are you?"

"I'm fine," she said.

"Barely, apparently."

"What do you mean?"

"What do you mean, 'what do you mean?'"

"I mean, I just woke up and suddenly the world is texting and calling me."

He sighed. "Then it wasn't you."

"What wasn't me?"

"Have you seen the Internet this morning?"

"No, why?"

"Because you and Derek have taken it over."

The first glimmerings of what apparently had transpired began to dawn on her. "What is the Internet saying?"

"So many things, my dear, so many things. Let us see...." He paused, and she imagined him scrolling and clicking through different websites. "You were trapped on a mountain in a dangerous ice storm, the roads treacherous and impassable. Derek rescued you — by helicopter, of all things. Very dramatic, like something out of one of his movies. You two are back together. No, wait, you aren't back together yet, but he's determined to win you back. He saved your life. You're beyond grateful. You think he's dashing and heroic. The two of you are destined to be together. The Hollywood action star and the Broadway beauty. I'm sure you get the picture."

Melody sighed, trying to push back the boulder of tension that had just rolled onto her stomach. "Nigel, I'm sorry. I had no idea."

"My dear, when the biggest movie star in the world follows you into the northern wilderness, *word will get out*. When that happens, I need to know so that I can do my job for you."

"You're right. I'm sorry. I should have told you yesterday."

"So what exactly did happen, my dear?" Now that he'd expressed his irritation with the situation and with her, his clipped tones began to soften. "Are you truly all right?"

"Yes, I'm fine." Briefly, she recapped her previous two days.

"Then, strictly speaking, the reporting about the helicopter is accurate," he said with a sigh.

"That part, yes," she said. "He arrived in a helicopter. I left with him by helicopter."

"The usuals are calling for comment. What do we tell them?"

She took a deep breath. "Keep it general and upbeat. I'm grateful to Derek and appreciate his help."

"And about the two of you?"

"Nothing. Leave that alone. Though in the spirit of full disclosure, I did agree to have coffee with him today."

"Ah, the promised coffee date. May I ask why you agreed to that?"

"Because he asked. In the helicopter. After all the trouble he went to, I couldn't really refuse."

She heard him exhale heavily. He didn't do that often. When he did, it usually meant he was preparing to venture into territory he preferred to avoid.

"My dear," he said, "you know I respect and adore you as an intelligent, emotionally aware woman who is fully capable of making her own important life decisions."

She felt a smile coming on. *Really, he was such a dear.* "But you want to tell me what to do."

"I do."

"Please go ahead."

"You'll ignore me if you disagree?"

"As always."

"Very well." He took another deep breath, then continued. "The story is getting huge play. The public is responding in a very positive way. If you want, we can leverage the attention to your benefit."

He paused. She almost jumped into the silence, but instead waited.

Finally, she heard him take another deep breath. "But I do not recommend that."

"Because of ... Derek?"

"No. Or rather, not because of who he is as a person. I believe him to be a basically decent chap. He doesn't always make the right choices — letting you go was an error, for example — but no one is perfect. All of us make mistakes."

"Then your recommendation is...."

"More about you."

"Me?" she said, surprised.

"You are more than a client to me, my dear. You are my friend. I want you to be happy."

"And for me to be happy...."

"I recommend you decline his request for a do-over."

She blinked. "Why?"

"Because his world isn't yours, my dear, at least not any longer. He's a deal-maker now, a mogul, far more than he is an actor. He operates on a very different level. His most important conversations are about power and money. I don't want that world for you."

"Why?" she asked, keeping her tone neutral, thoroughly unsure what to think and feel about what she was hearing.

"His world is glamorous, fast-paced, exciting, even momentous. If you were to choose to embrace that life, I have no doubt you would quickly excel at it. But there is a downside to his world. It takes over. It consumes all. It would, at the very least, distract you from your true calling."

"My true calling?"

He cleared his throat, then continued. "You, my dear, are an actor, a singer, an entertainer, an artist — one of uncommon ability. You have found a voice and a home in a community that embraces and celebrates artistic achievement and the hard work that goes into that. Your happiness lies in that world, not in his."

She swallowed, surprised again. "I'm not sure what to say."

"I want you to promise me, in the days ahead,

that you will keep your focus on *you* and what matters most to *you*."

"Nigel," she said softly, "you really are a dear."

"I can be," he allowed. "Don't you forget it."

She laughed.

"Of course, if you find yourself dazzled and decide to give him a second shot, I will do my very best to help you navigate."

"Thank you."

"All right, that's far too much unsolicited advice for one day. Is there anything non-Derek-related that I need to be made aware of?"

I met someone, she almost said, but held back. Nigel would demand to know more. He'd ask questions. He'd want answers.

Answers that I want, too.

"You'll be the first to hear."

"Exactly what I hoped you'd say."

Her phone vibrated again. "Darling, I'm getting inundated with texts. I need to let everyone know I'm fine."

"And I must feed the ravenous media beast."

"Nigel, I hope you have a wonderful Christmas. Give my best to Pamela and the kids."

"You, too, dear. I wish you and your mother a most merry and happy Christmas."

CHAPTER 28

*N*inety minutes later, with a glance in her bathroom mirror, Melody gave her reflection a final inspection before heading out. Yes, she confirmed, she was appropriately dressed for her coffee date with Derek — not too dressed up, but not too casual either. Her dark jeans, sleek burgundy cashmere sweater, simple gold hoop earrings — all of those looked good. The foundation and mascara applied lightly but carefully — also good. Her hair, rich and red and lustrous — actually quite good.

She added a final dab of lip gloss, then nodded and headed out.

Derek was waiting for her at the foot of the stairs. He gazed up appreciatively as she made her way down.

"Morning," he said. "You look great."

"Thank you. So do you."

Which was nothing but the honest truth. Derek was one of those rare people who, very annoyingly, always managed to look terrific. He could show up in a tux at the beach, or in gym clothes at a gala, and still somehow make it work. Today he was in his usual jeans and fitted grey sweater, with a dark grey overcoat and a blue scarf. He looked alert and rested and raring to go.

But also, perhaps, a bit nervous? Had she caught a glimpse of something — she couldn't be sure — behind his confident gaze?

"It's lovely outside," Melody said. "Let's walk to the cafe."

"After you," he said, ushering her out.

The sky was clear and blue, a hint of a breeze stirring the crisp morning air. A light blanket of snow covered the roofs and lawns and trees.

As they walked, she did her best to keep the conversation on safe topics. She asked about his upcoming projects, interspersing her questions with tidbits about the shops they passed. When they reached the bandstand in the heart of the town square, she said, "Every year, a night or two before Christmas, the town gathers here for the annual caroling concert."

He glanced at the bandstand. "You ever take part?"

"Two years ago," she said, choosing not to add,

right after you dumped me. "And I'll be joining this year as well."

He pointed ahead. "Is that our destination?"

She followed his gaze to the Heartsprings Valley Cafe, its big windows and Christmas decorations beckoning. "The best scones and lattes in town."

After crossing the street, Derek held open the door. "After you."

A smile came to her lips as she stepped inside, the lovely, familiar aromas filling her with warmth and reassurance. Though the morning rush was over, half the tables were still occupied and a short line of customers stood at the counter, waiting to place their orders.

As she and Derek got in line, she was aware that the usual glancing and whispering had begun. Being spotted in public by fans was a reality for both of them, though far more so for Derek. Melody often got away with not being recognized, and she was now a familiar-enough presence in Heartsprings Valley that her comings and goings didn't warrant undue interest.

But the arrival in town of one of the planet's most famous faces — that was a different story. Given the speed and efficiency of the local grapevine, Melody bet most of the town was already well aware that Derek Davies was in town.

And very soon everyone would know he was here. At the cafe!

They reached the counter. Holly wasn't there — perhaps she was in the back? Instead, at the register was a young woman, aged eighteen or so, tall and lanky with long blond hair, whose eyes lit up with excitement when she realized who they were.

"Omigosh," the young woman said. "Both of you, right here. I read what happened. Mr. Davies, I'm Eva, and I'm a huge fan!"

"Pleased to meet you, Eva," Derek said.

Eva turned to Melody. "Ms. Connelly, I know you're moving here, and I love your songs!"

"Thank you, darling. So pleased to meet you."

"Are you two getting back together?"

The question came as a shock, though it shouldn't have, not after what the Internet had just announced. Clearly, this Eva was an enthusiastic and informed young woman who didn't hold back when it came to asking probing questions.

Derek, an old pro when it came to deflecting the same, turned up the charm. "Well, we stopped in to have coffee." Then he leaned closer and said conspiratorially, "But what I hear is that you have the best scones in town."

"Oh, definitely," Eva said. "They're super-delicious. Holly — she's my boss — came up with all the recipes."

"How's the bacon-apple scone?"

"It's awesome."

"Then based on your recommendation, Eva, I would love a bacon-apple scone and a large coffee."

Melody added, "And an apple-cranberry scone and a mocha latte for me."

"Got it," Eva said, typing in their order. But then a cloud passed over her face. "Do I ask too many questions?" she blurted out. "I know what I asked isn't really any of my business, and sometimes people tell me to put a lid on it — not you, you guys were really nice about it — but how can I put a lid on it when people are already saying the same stuff and I just want to know if what they're saying is right?"

Melody couldn't help but smile. This young woman's earnestness was so *adorable*. "What I would say is, as long as your questions are coming from a good place, keep asking. Perhaps you'll become a reporter someday?"

Eva's eyes widened. "Yes! That's my dream job. How did you know?"

"Just a guess."

Eva beamed. "Okay, let me get your order."

While they waited, Derek turned to Melody, a sheepish look in his eyes, and said quietly, "You saw what's out?"

She nodded. "I did."

"Sorry about that."

"No worries."

Eva finished up their order. "I hope you both have a very merry Christmas!"

"Very nice to meet you, Eva," Melody said. "Merry Christmas to you."

Coffees and scones in hand, they made their way to an open table next to one of the big windows facing the town square.

After settling in, Derek took a test bite of his scone and chewed. His eyes widened in surprise. "This is really good," he said, then took a bigger bite.

"Holly has a gift," Melody said.

She took a sip of her mocha and prepared herself for what was coming. This was the moment Derek had asked for three days earlier, and the moment she'd agreed to yesterday. She knew him well enough to know that his silence wouldn't last long. Derek didn't tend to hold back. When he wanted something, he went for it. When he had something to say, he said it.

"So," he said, setting down his scone and giving her his undivided attention. "I'm really very glad you agreed to have coffee with me."

"I'm glad to do it."

"I want us to give us another shot," he said, leaning forward, ramping up the intensity of his movie-star gaze. "I was a fool to break up with you, Melody. A total idiot. I never should have let you go. I know that now."

She swallowed, feeling again how powerfully persuasive he could be when he dialed up the charm.

"That's why I came up here," he continued.

"Totally unplanned, totally spur-of-the-moment. I just got in a car and drove. Because I had to tell you how sorry I am. And show you how I feel."

She realized, as she held his magnetic gaze, that she really could fall for him again. The edge of the precipice was right in front of her, just a step or two away.

She had to pull back. Before she did a thing, she had to know, to *feel*, what was right. And she didn't know that yet. Or did she?

She cleared her throat. "You must be missing things in New York — events, appearances, meetings."

He waved them away. "Nothing important."

"Nigel called and kind of chewed me out this morning. He saw the news about you and me and the storm and the helicopter and wanted to know what in the world was going on."

"I'm sorry about that," he said, giving her a *what-can-you-do-about-those-pesky-media-types* look. "I told my people about the storm but didn't tell them to keep it quiet, so they ran with it."

She sighed. "It's fine. A bit dramatic, though, some of it."

He shrugged. "You know how it goes."

"Yes, I most certainly do."

"If anything, the attention proves I'm not the only one who wants us to have another shot."

Her brow furrowed. "What do you mean?"

"Our fans want it, too. One little news story and — *boom.*"

He was right about that. Nigel had said much the same.

"The story they're telling about me," he continued, "is that two years ago Derek Davies was an idiot and had no clue, but now he gets it."

"And the story they're telling about Melody Connelly?"

"Easily the more interesting story," he said, leaning forward. "But one that only she can tell."

She swallowed, unsure how to respond.

He bit his lower lip, just briefly. From experience, she knew he'd just made a decision.

"Can I ask you a direct question?" he said.

"Of course."

"You know me. No beating around the bush."

"Ask away."

"Your new friend James. The furniture guy."

"James?" she repeated, color rising to her cheeks.

"Is something going on with you two?"

"Why would you say that?" she said, instinctively trying to buy time. "We just met."

He didn't say anything, regarding her steadily.

"Why the look?" she asked.

"Yesterday, at the house, I sensed a connection."

"A connection?"

"It got me worried."

"Derek," she said, reaching out to give his hand a

quick pat, "you should be worried about my feelings for *you*."

"Ah," he said, leaning back. "Moment of truth."

"Yes, darling, moment of truth." She pausing, trying to find the right words. Across the table, her former beau tensed, like he was preparing for the worst.

"The truth is," she said, "two years ago, when you ended things with me, I was hurt. I had hopes for our relationship, and those hopes were dashed when you broke us up." She took a deep breath. "But here's what I've learned. I've learned that time really does heal. I've learned I can sit with you in a lovely cafe and enjoy a lovely mocha and not have the past intrude. I can be here with you and experience this moment *in this moment*. I'm glad about that."

"I'm glad, too," he said cautiously.

She picked up her latte, appreciating its warmth in her hands. "So here we are, in this moment, two years later. You tell me you want to go back to what we had. I truly appreciate you saying that. But for me, there's no going back. There's only moving forward. Do you understand what I'm saying?"

He didn't answer right away, then cleared his throat. "You're looking for a fresh start."

She nodded. "Yes, that's exactly right. A fresh start in every way."

"Meaning … what?"

"Well … that is an excellent question." She

stopped, her mind suddenly racing. She didn't know why, but like a bolt out of the blue, she knew what she had to do.

She set her latte down. "I can't give you an answer right now, Derek. But I will be able to — soon. I promise."

"Okay," he said, taken aback.

"I'm hosting a Christmas party at my new house tomorrow evening." The words coming out of her mouth surprised her, but she pushed on. "The house is still unfinished and nothing's been moved in and the gathering is very impromptu — I decided just now to do it — but I don't care. Oh, gosh, there's so much to do. I'd love to have you attend. Can you stick around?"

He nodded. "Sure, I can do that."

"Good. I'm glad."

A silence followed. By unspoken agreement, they allowed the moment to linger. The quiet wasn't comfortable, but neither was it unpleasant. Somehow, the silence felt necessary.

Derek took a sip of coffee, his gaze thoughtful. Then he set his cup down. "Different topic. Can I ask you something?"

"Sure."

"What's the deal with this town?"

Melody managed — barely — to not burst out laughing. "What do you mean?"

Derek looked perplexed. "Somehow — I have no

idea how this happened — I got roped into a fund-raising event tonight by a guy who showed up at the Inn this morning. A guy named Bert?"

"Bert Winters? The mayor? Looks like Santa's younger brother?"

"That's him. He's oddly persuasive. One minute he's telling me about the town's annual Christmas charity drive, and the next minute I'm agreeing to host a showing of one of my films at the local high school."

Melody smiled. "Bert's a wonder."

"So that's where I'll be tonight."

"At the high school. Hosting a film showing."

"Live and in person."

"You'll introduce the film? Do a Q&A?"

"Yeah, the usual."

"Which film?"

"Don't know. He said he'll pick it. I just have to show up and talk."

"This town has a way of pulling you in." Melody spread her arms wide, encouraging Derek to take in the sights and appreciate their surroundings. "I've learned to roll with it, darling. Welcome to Heart-springs Valley!"

CHAPTER 29

*E*arly the following morning, Melody stood on the front porch of her beautiful Victorian home, list in hand, enjoying the crisp winter air and the first rays of sun on her cheeks. She glanced again at the piece of paper she'd used to write down her first actual to-do list in ages. She scanned the tasks, most of them crossed off, and allowed herself a small pat on the back.

Yes, she was ready.

Sort of.

Mostly.

Though also a bit crazed, she acknowledged. Channeling her inner Clara meant recognizing that Melody-the-dreamer could be a bit of a challenge every now and then. Dreaming big dreams meant a ton of work for those who organized those dreams into existence.

Which in this case was — mostly herself.

Since her sudden inspiration in the cafe the previous day, she'd been a whirlwind of activity. With the enthusiastic help of her mom and Benny, she'd leaped into action, activating multitasking muscles she hadn't used since her days as a struggling waitress-singer-actress.

In the kitchen, her big new coffee machine was busy brewing coffee on the counter, next to the heaping pile of scones and muffins and croissants she'd just picked up from Holly at the cafe.

In her hand were party invitations, printed the previous evening at the hardware store, which she would soon be passing out.

She and Luke had discussed the day's plan of attack, and he'd texted a few minutes ago that he was on his way.

Through the trees, she heard the rumble of an engine. A few seconds later, a small truck appeared, Luke behind the wheel, two guys in the front seat with him. He parked in front of the house and jumped out.

"Morning, Melody!"

"Morning, Luke!"

The two men hopped out with him, and Melody stepped forward as Luke made the introductions.

"Thank you for your help today moving everything in," she said as she handed each of them an invitation. "I hope you can attend. Very last-minute, very casual, tonight from six to nine. Please invite your family and friends. I would love to meet my new neighbors."

Luke smiled as he scanned the invite. "'Camping at Christmas,'" he read out loud. "'Please join for a casual, impromptu celebration of the holiday spirit.'"

"I knew I'd have to keep things simple, given the current state of the house."

He gestured to the truck. "As discussed, we're starting with the living room."

"Perfect," she said, glancing toward the woods as a second truck emerged from the woods. "There are treats and coffee for everyone in the kitchen. Please help yourselves — and don't be shy!"

"Great." Luke turned to his crew. "Guys, let's get to it."

And then they were off.

The hours that followed flew by in a blur as trucks were unloaded and furniture and boxes were carried inside by Luke's team. As promised, the furniture and boxes for the living room arrived first — which was important, given that the party would take place in that room in a matter of hours. The sounds of footsteps on stairs and men saying things like "a little to the left" and "hang on while I shift" filled the house.

At one point, while Melody was in the living room getting ready to open a box that she hoped

contained a table lamp, she looked up and found
James smiling at her.

"Good morning!" she said, very aware of the jolt
coursing through her at the sight of him.

"Morning," he replied. "Hard at it, I see."

If the spark in his grey eyes was any indication,
he was just as happy to see her. He was dressed in his
typical work outfit of jeans, flannel shirt, and work
boots.

She waved her arm around the room, now filled
with boxes and furniture. "Madness, I know."

Then she remembered — *the invitation!*

She stood up, grabbed one, and handed it
to him.

He scanned it, a grin transforming his face.
"'Camping at Christmas?'"

"You and Anna simply must come."

"Of course. Anna will be thrilled." His gaze swept
the room. "Where's the tree going?"

She pointed to a spot in front of the big rear-
facing windows. "There. In the place of honor."

"You need help bringing it in?"

"That would be great."

They made their way out to the front porch,
standing aside as two movers brought in a mattress,
then reached down and grabbed hold of the tree.
After two nights outside on the porch, the branches
were cold to the touch. The scent of fresh evergreen
filled her nostrils.

"Most of the water dripped away, which is good," he said. "You ready?"

"Ready."

"One, two, three, lift." They stood up together and, after shifting into a comfortable position, James guided them back inside. The tree was heavier than she'd remembered — she'd picked a big one! — and maneuvering it through the maze of furniture and boxes took some doing, but they managed to get it across the room.

They set it down, leaning it temporarily next to the fireplace, and James looked around. "Where's the box from Abner?"

She thought for a moment. "The kitchen. I'll get it."

He gestured to the tree. "And I'll unwrap the twine."

In the kitchen, she spied the box she was after. It seemed right — appropriate, even — that it was James helping with this particular task. After all, he'd been with her when she'd impulsively decided she needed to get a tree just moments before a major storm. And now here he was again, helping her bring the tree inside and into its intended place....

She returned to the living room with Abner's box and heard a familiar "Yoo-hoo!" She looked over her shoulder. Her mom and Benny had arrived.

"Oh, what a nice big tree!" her mom said. "Good to see you again, James."

James gave them a big grin. "Good to see you two."

Benny clapped his hands together. "We're here to help. What do you need?"

"I think we should be good," James said. "Melody, if you could place the tree stand where you want the tree…."

"Got it." She took the stand, set it on the ground, then stood up to double-check. It was almost in the right spot, but not quite. She moved it a few inches to the left, then backed up again and glanced at her mom, who nodded confirmation.

"Ready?" James said.

"Ready."

Wrapping his long arms around the tree, he picked it up, moved it to the stand, and carefully lowered it in. Free of the twine, the branches looked so full and bushy — she'd definitely picked the right one.

"How does it look?" James asked.

"It looks great."

"I'll need you to hold it in place while I fasten it in."

She reached deep into the tree and grabbed hold, the evergreen scent filling her lungs, while James dropped to the floor and tightened the screws holding the tree in place.

"You two got this down," Benny said approvingly. "A well-oiled machine."

"Indeed," her mom murmured.

Melody glanced over, instantly aware of what her mom was really saying. There was a gentle smile on her mom's face and an encouraging gleam in her eyes.

Once again Melody felt her cheeks turning pink, but she resisted the urge to protest. Because really, what was the point? Barely in town two days, already her mom had embraced Heartsprings Valley's pro-meddling stance.

No, the better course of action was to distract and divert. "Mom, I was thinking that you and Benny and I could focus on getting this room unpacked and decorated for the party."

"Of course, darling."

"Whatever you need." Benny added.

From below, she heard James say, "Okay, let's see if the tree's fastened tight enough."

"Should I let go?"

"Yes, but stay close in case it slips."

She let go of the tree but didn't move her arm. The tree stayed upright.

"You let go?" James asked.

"It's standing up on its own."

"Give it a bit of a push. A gentle one."

She did as requested and was pleased to see the tree remain firmly upright.

"One more time, from a different angle."

She repeated the push, this time slightly harder.

Still no movement. *Hurray!*

"I think you've done it," Melody said.

James stood up, brushed a few needles from his hands, then stepped back and gave the tree a final inspection. He nodded with approval. "You'll probably need to tighten or adjust the screws every couple of days."

"No problem."

"What's the decorating plan?"

"I picked up tons of ornaments and lights from the hardware store. We'll start with the lighting and go on from there."

"If you need anything, I'm happy to help." He paused, looking around the room. "You've got a lot of work in here. I was planning to push on the trim work — the end's in sight on that — but if you'd prefer, I could...."

"Oh, thank you, but no need. Mom and Benny and I will manage."

He smiled at her, his gaze holding hers. "You know where I am. You need anything, just holler."

She felt it then — the same pull, the same impulse to step toward him, the same desire to pull him close, to —

"I'll holler," she managed to say.

"Okay," he said, seemingly unwilling to move. Then he blinked, looked toward her mom and Benny, and stepped away. "See you in a bit?"

Melody swallowed. "Most definitely."

With a lingering glance, he headed for the media room.

When Melody turned, she found her mom and Benny staring at her unabashedly, big knowing grins on their faces.

"Mom. Not now. Please?"

After a short pause, her mom relented. "But soon."

Melody felt a surge of emotion rushing through her — a surge that was both exhilarating and a bit unnerving. "We have a party to plan. You ready?"

Her mom rubbed her hands together. "Darling, let's do it!"

CHAPTER 30

Far too quickly and almost before they knew it, it was party time!

Melody cast a glance around at the living room, scarcely able to believe the transformation. Gone forever was the empty room with nothing in it but two couches. In just a few short hours, the couches had been turned into anchors for a conversational grouping positioned in front of the fireplace, joined by a lovely Oriental rug, side tables, a coffee table, and table lamps that cast a warm glow. Across the room, a second conversation area featured a pair of smaller two-seater sofas, and against the walls were long storage cabinets.

But what really set her heart singing were the Christmas decorations. She and her mom and Benny hadn't held back. Holiday touches were everywhere: an evergreen wreath above the fireplace mantel, a statue of Santa and his reindeer on a sideboard, jars of tempting candy canes throughout the room, plates heaped with Christmas cookies on the coffee table, and strings of brightly colored lights lining the big windows. In its place of honor, her beautiful Christmas tree boasted oodles of bright lights and a gorgeous silver star that nearly brushed the ceiling.

With an abundance of candles lighting up the mantel and a fireplace throwing lovely heat into the room, the space felt wonderful. Like Christmas.

Her mom stepped to her side, glowing with satisfaction. "We did it."

Melody pulled her mom in for a hug. "Thank you."

Her mom returned the hug. "I meant what I said earlier."

Melody's brow furrowed. "Meant what?"

"About it being time soon."

The phrasing was cryptic, but Melody understood. "Mom, I —"

"Soon, darling."

A sound came that Melody realized she was hearing for the first time: the chiming of her new doorbell. It was like a bell, clear and cheerful, announcing —

"Our first guests!" Melody said. "How do we look?"

They gave each other a quick once-over. Melody had changed into black slacks and an emerald green silk blouse that, from experience, she knew worked well with her hair, accompanied by gold hoop earrings and a cute faux-jeweled snowman broach she'd picked up at the hardware store. Her mom had changed into a lovely navy-blue dress, with a red ruby necklace adding a dash of color.

"You look terrific," her mom said.

"So do you."

"You ready?"

"Let's do it."

Melody opened the front door and found the town's mayor, Bert Winters, accompanied by his wife Elsie. The two of them looked like everyone's favorite grandparents and were dressed in exuberant Christmas sweaters.

"Mr. Mayor and Elsie, welcome and Merry Christmas!" Melody said.

"Melody, thank you for having us," the mayor said. "Merry Christmas!"

After introducing them to her mom, Melody handed each a tree ornament. "We're asking each guest to help decorate the tree."

"Oh, that sounds wonderful," Elsie said.

"Tonight's theme is all about camping — because that's what I did here the other night during the storm. There's hot cocoa in the kitchen, plus popcorn and licorice and candy bars and more, plus lots of treats from Holly's cafe, and later on we'll have s'mores by the fire."

The mayor looked around the restored foyer with pride and satisfaction. "Melody, on behalf of everyone in town, thank you for taking on the challenge of restoring this old place and bringing it back to life."

"Oh, gosh," she replied with a laugh. "The biggest thanks go to Luke and his team. They did the work, not me."

"But the inspiration, the driving force — that was you."

Elsie added, "We couldn't be happier about you becoming part of the community here in Heartsprings Valley."

Melody felt a surge of affection. "I'm glad, too. Please, enjoy yourselves!"

As more folks flowed in, Melody and her mom made sure to greet each arrival with a smile and an ornament.

When James and Anna arrived, Melody found she couldn't wipe the smile from her face.

"Ms. Connelly," Anna said, "thank you for inviting us."

"Please, you must call me *Melody*."

"Okay," Anna said with a delighted laugh. "*Melody!*"

"I'd like to introduce you to my mom."

As the two women exchanged greetings, Melody glanced at James and found him gazing intently at her. He liked that she and Anna liked each other, she could tell. Very clearly, he liked that *a lot.*

He'd dressed up, she noted — black slacks and a blue collared dress shirt that complemented his grey eyes.

She flushed as she suddenly flashed to their first evening together, to the two of them standing in this very spot in the foyer, dripping wet from freezing rain. She almost wanted to go back to that moment and be alone with him again, beginning their adventure, learning about each other, opening herself to feelings and possibilities she'd always shied away from….

A gust of winter air flowed in and she blinked. Three new arrivals stood in the doorway: Derek, Barbara, and Stu.

"Welcome!" her mom said. "Merry Christmas!"

James tensed slightly at the sight of Derek. But the smile didn't leave his face as he turned to Melody and said, "We'll see you inside in a bit?"

"Yes, of course, but don't forget these," Melody said, handing ornaments to him and Anna. "I need your help decorating the tree."

With more guests right behind Derek, Barbara, and Stu, Melody was again swept up in a rush of greetings and introductions and welcomes. It didn't take long for the house to fill with guests.

"Darling," her mom said as the flow slowed, "it

feels like most folks are here. You should circulate. I'll handle the late arrivals."

"You sure?"

"Of course."

"Thank you," she said, realizing again how grateful she was to have her mom here with her. "For everything. I mean it."

Her mom blinked, startled but clearly pleased. "There's nowhere else I'd rather be."

"I want to make this our best Christmas ever."

"Oh, my darling girl," her mom said, her voice softening. "It already is."

Melody felt it then — a rush of feeling, with tears not far behind. But now was not the moment for that!

"I'm so glad to hear that, Mom." She swallowed, doing all she could to push back the wave of emotion. "That's my dream for us this Christmas."

"Darling," her mom said, as if filled with a sudden resolve, "there's something I've been wanting to talk with you about."

"What's that, Mom?"

Before her mom could say more, the doorbell rang again. "Duty calls," her mom said. "You go circulate. I'll find you."

Curious but accepting that now was not the time, Melody did as her mom suggested, wading into the living room and embracing her role as hostess. Gosh, there were a lot of people — fifty, sixty? – but the room seemed to hold them just fine. How wonderful that this grand old house was once again alive with conversation and laughter. The lovely aromas of peppermint hot chocolate and hot apple cider filled the air. She spied Benny circulating with trays of cookies and wasn't surprised to see Barbara pitching in as well.

Across the room, she noticed Derek slip into the dining room, his attention apparently drawn by something. Curious, Melody slipped through the crowd and found him admiring her new dining table, his fingers lightly tracing the live edge.

He glanced at her. "Your friend James is very talented." The words came reluctantly, like he would have preferred encountering a lesser level of craftsmanship. "Half the people I know would kill to have this piece in their homes."

"I know," Melody said.

"And the other half — their loss." He turned to face her. "Thank you for inviting me tonight."

"I'm glad you're here," she said, pleased to discover she actually meant it. "I'm glad you came. I didn't realize how much I wanted — needed — this opportunity for a fresh start with you. I'm hopeful that, going forward, the past won't define our...."

She paused, looking for the right word.

At that moment, Benny popped his head in. "Melody, there you are. A question about the popcorn."

"Yes?"

"Folks want to make popcorn strings for the tree."

"Oh, that's wonderful!"

"And they're asking if we have thread…."

Thread! She thought for a moment. "We do. I can show you where." She turned to Derek. "Sorry, I have to…."

"No worries," he said. "Popcorn emergency. Go."

She grinned. "Thanks!"

It took a moment to find and open the box that had her sewing kit in it, but soon enough she was back in the living room and handing Benny needles and spools of thread. Her attention was caught by her Christmas tree, now bursting with ornaments. It looked lovely — and its branches so full. Thank goodness she'd picked a big, bushy, sturdy specimen.

She blinked as her gaze landed on an ornament she hadn't bought. Where had it come from? Had a guest brought it? She leaned in to examine it. It was hand-carved wood, about the size and shape of a Christmas cookie, and depicted two birds on a branch, entwined. A light lacquer finish brought out the natural grains of the wood.

There was artistry here, and not just in the choice of wood. Almost reverently, she plucked it off the tree and ran her fingers over it. The curves used to define the birds, the flow of the two of them nestled together, the delicate yet sure touch — there was beauty in this piece, along with the power to evoke an emotional response.

A voice at her side said, "The birds are turtledoves."

Startled, Melody swiveled and found Anna.

"Sorry," the young woman said. "Didn't mean to sneak up on you."

"Oh, no worries." Melody returned the ornament to its spot on the tree. "How do you know what kind of birds they are?"

"Dad told me."

Melody blinked, surprised. "Your dad?"

"He told me when he was making it."

A surge of emotion hit her. "Your dad made this?"

"Last night, while we were at home, watching TV. It's one of his specialties."

"One of his specialties?"

"Sculpting pieces like this. He's always whittling away at something. This time of year, it's usually a tree ornament. He gives the ornaments away as Christmas presents."

Melody's amazement grew. The ornament now hanging on her tree seemed effortlessly beautiful — simple, soulful, and perfect. "You're telling me he made this *last night*?"

Anna nodded. "He added the shellac or lacquer — I'm never sure what to call it — this morning. He carves them pretty fast. A few hours, tops. It kind of just flows out of him. Like he knows what the wood wants to be."

Melody nodded. "Like he hears what the wood is saying. Like he's tuned into it."

Anna's brow furrowed. "Yes, exactly. How did you...."

"We were talking along similar lines the other night."

Anna glanced across the room, where James was in conversation with Benny. "You like him, don't you?"

Melody swallowed, taken aback, then surprised herself by admitting, "Yes, I do."

"But you also have feelings for your ex."

It came out as a statement, not a question. Before Melody could reply, Anna said, "I mean, I know I would. Just look at him." She gestured to the other side of the room, where Derek was talking with the mayor. "He's gorgeous!"

Melody smiled. "That he is."

"I guess what I'm saying is don't leave them hanging. Either of them."

"You really are a remarkable young woman. And you're exactly right. I promise I'll do my best."

"Thank you."

"But going back to the ornaments for the moment...."

"Yes?"

"Are all of your dad's ornaments this good?"

Anna nodded. "Oh, sure, absolutely. I mean, I'm biased, but I'm also kind of a Christmas ornament freak and I know what's out there, and Dad's measure up to anyone's."

Melody nodded. She'd figured as much. "Has he thought about turning them into...."

"A business? Selling them on his website?"

"Yes."

"No, he hasn't," Anna said, irritation in her tone, "which is so frustrating, because I've been bugging and bugging him to try!"

"Darling, I'm happy to lend my voice. With the right marketing push, I could see these doing very well."

Anna beamed at her. "We can be allies in the cause?"

Melody chuckled. "Will your father forgive us if we gang up on him?"

Anna laughed. "He won't have a choice."

Melody laughed with her. "Then count me in."

At that moment, her mom joined them. "Anna, darling, there you are."

"You need me for something?"

"The mayor had a question about your research into the town's history?"

"Then I'd better get over here." With a smile, Anna slipped away.

"She's a wonderful young woman," Melody said.

"That she is." Her mom turned to her. "Melody, darling." She took a deep breath. "Before I lose my nerve, can we talk?"

CHAPTER 31

*M*elody blinked, the question taking her by surprise.

"Talk, Mom?"

Her mom took a deep breath, as if fortifying herself. "Yes."

"Of course. About what?"

Another deep breath. "Something I've wanted to talk about for a long time."

"What's that?"

"Our mistakes."

Melody's stomach clenched. "Our mistakes?"

"Mine and yours."

With the words finally out, there was an assurance in her mom's tone that Melody couldn't help but respond to. "Sure."

Her mom took her hand. "It's quieter in the

study." Together, they slipped through the crowd in the living room and into the smaller room, which was still empty except for unpacked boxes in a corner.

"Specifically," her mom said, shutting the door behind them, "I want to talk about two big mistakes that define us."

Through the closed door, the sounds of the party had become muffled. Her mom's voice, though soft, was steady and clear.

Two big mistakes that define us. An interesting statement. Melody girded herself for what was coming. No, that wasn't right — *girded herself* didn't truly capture the complicated mix of emotions she was experiencing. There was tension, even anxiety, coursing through her, yes. But the bigger part of her wanted to know, needed to know, what her mom had chosen in this moment to share, and why.

"Mom, I'm not sure what you mean, but I want to find out."

"I'm glad to hear that," her mom said, then took a deep breath, revealing her nervousness as well. "This is something I've wanted to talk about with you for a long time. But maybe I should have waited until after the party."

"No, you took action. That's a good thing."

Her mom reached out to take her hands again. "Yes, that's exactly right. Taking action is a good thing." She took a deep breath. "My darling girl, before I say what I want to say, I want you to know how proud I am of you. Even as a little girl, you had such determination. You took your natural gifts and made something of yourself. You grew up to become an amazing woman. So talented, so brave, so hard-working."

Tears came to Melody's eyes. "Mom...."

"I'm not done, dear. You are so strong. A power-house! Stronger than I've ever been. And a dreamer! You never let your fears hold you back. Except...."

"Except?"

"Except when it comes to love."

Melody felt her throat constrict.

Her mom squeezed her hands. "Before I say more, I need to take a detour. I want to tell you about my big mistake, one that helps define *me*. I'm sure you know what it is, but I want to say it out loud, right now, with you."

Melody found herself trembling. "And your big mistake is...?"

"My big mistake is, I leap before I look."

Her mom looked so nervous all of a sudden — vulnerable yet determined at the same time.

"Mom, I'm glad you said that." The words weren't a surprise, but having her say them aloud to her — that meant something. "I think I know what my big mistake is."

Her mom swallowed. "Your mistake is, you don't leap. At least not when it comes to love."

"Mom...."

"Hush, darling, let your mother talk. Oh, I hope this comes out right." She took another deep breath and continued. "I'm thinking about that boy Davey you dated in high school. A nice boy. I liked him a lot. I heard he grew up to be a fine man. You and he would have been good together. But you ended things with him before you could find out."

"I wasn't ready," Melody said.

"I agree, you weren't. Then, a few years after you moved to New York, you met that fellow. That young architect."

"Darren." Her lip trembled at the memory.

"He really loved you."

"And I him. But we wanted different things."

"Maybe so. But again, you ended things with him before the two of you could find out how different those things really were."

"Mom, I...."

"And then there's Derek." Her mom paused, glancing at the closed door to make sure no one could overhear. "He's a special case, being a big star and all. You got swept up in the rush, didn't you? Dating someone like him is a completely different experience, isn't it?"

Melody nodded. "I got swept."

"And he ended things. Not you."

"That's right."

"And that's important. For the first time, *you*

didn't end things. Instead you leaped — or at least, you were ready to leap. I know it hurt when he broke things off. But the breakup showed you something important. It proved you're strong enough to recover and move forward."

"I take it you had doubts."

"No, darling. But I think *you* did."

Before Melody could respond, her mom reached up and gripped her shoulders. There was a strength in her grip, a determination, that Melody saw all too rarely. From the expression on her mom's face, it was clear she felt this moment was important.

Her mom swallowed. "What I'm saying, dear, is that I'm sorry. For all of it."

"Sorry for what?"

"Your dating history. It's my fault. You saw the messes I jumped into and decided to do the very opposite."

"Mom, I...."

"I want you to listen to your mother." She took a step back and, after a pause, continued. "Some people are lucky in love. They leap and land like fate is guiding them. They meet the right person and know it. For the rest of us — and that includes you and me — love means taking a chance and leaping and falling flat on our faces, time and time again. We don't stick the landing the first time or two or three, because the landing is actually quicksand or too rocky or — you get what I'm trying to say, right?"

Melody smiled. "Yes, Mom, I get it."

"For us, love means getting up and dusting ourselves off and leaping again."

"Until we land on our feet."

"Which I finally did, with Benny. I am so glad I found him."

"It took a while, didn't it?"

"Far too long. But you know what? I'm grateful for my mistaken leaps. Each and every one." She sighed. "Okay, that's not true. A couple of the guys I picked — what in the world was I thinking?"

"You mean, like Jim?"

Her mom let out a short laugh and shook her head. "Oh, he's a nice man. But sail around the world? Me?"

"I'm glad you got off that boat and flew home."

"So am I, darling, so am I." She took Melody's hands in hers. "But I firmly believe I was meant to make my mistakes — to experience them and learn from them. Like the universe was getting me ready for what I have now."

The universe. Melody felt its presence at her shoulder, listening closely, encouraging them both to express what they'd always been too hesitant or fearful to put into words.

"What I'm trying to say," her mom said, "is that I want you to leap. I know you're ready. I know you're strong enough. I want you to find and know the love you deserve."

The emotional rush tightening her throat took Melody by surprise. Tears threatened. Her mom looked so vulnerable staring up at her. The two of them had spent a lifetime either arguing with each other or tiptoeing around each other, anxious to avoid upsetting the other. The raw honesty of the moment was breathtaking.

Melody took a deep breath. "Now it's my turn to say something, Mom. I want to get this out, so please let me say what I want to say without interruption."

Her mom nodded, her gaze anxious yet hopeful.

Melody gave her mom's hands a squeeze. "I want to apologize for my mistakes. I was angry with you for a long time. But instead of reaching out and trying to work through our issues, I pushed you away."

"Oh, honey," her mom said, tears filling her eyes.

"For the longest time, I thought distance was the best way for me to deal with what I felt. I believed that creating boundaries would help me move past my disappointments and regrets. I thought I was being mature and grown-up and responsible. I thought it was best for me to keep you at arm's length."

A tear ran down her mother's face.

Swallowing, Melody continued. "On some level, at least for a while, I needed that distance. But in the past few years, I've felt that changing. Now I treasure how we're growing closer. When you came to New

York that long weekend after your cruise two years ago — when it was so cold we barely left my apartment? — I realized I no longer needed distance. What I needed instead was to put my heart and soul into mending our relationship."

"Oh, darling," her mom said, reaching out to pull her in for a hug.

"It means everything that you're here with me now, Mom." Melody wrapped her arms around her mother, surrendering to the warmth and security, feeling closer than she had in decades to this complicated yet loving woman. "I want you to know how much I love you and want you in my life."

"Oh, darling," her mom said, her voice soft in her ear. "I am so grateful. I want the same — I want it so much. I love you so much."

They allowed the hug to linger, the tears coming and flowing, relief and joy coursing through them like a river.

Finally, they pulled back and looked at each other and laughed.

"Look at us — total messes," her mom said.

Wiping her eyes, Melody said, "Bathroom — *stat.*"

They headed into the hallway bathroom and Melody handed her mom a handful of tissues. For a few seconds, the room was filled with the sounds of two women blowing their noses and returning themselves to a semblance of normalcy.

"No mirror?" her mom asked, looking at the space on the wall above the pedestal sink where the vanity would soon be.

"No," Melody said. "But soon."

They turned to examine each other's faces. Using fresh tissues, they brushed away each other's smudges.

"I like him, you know," her mom said.

"Do you?" Melody said, not needing to ask whom.

"I have a very good feeling about him."

Melody felt a tremor run through her. "So do I."

"Of course, I think the other one's pretty good, too."

"Do you?"

"I do."

Melody didn't reply. Her well of emotion, barely suppressed, threatened to overwhelm her again.

"You have a decision to make," her mom said.

Melody tensed. "I do."

"A chance to take."

"I do."

"A leap to make."

She nodded, a lump forming in her throat. "I do."

"Are you ready?"

"I don't know."

"Not good enough." Her mom took hold of her shoulders. "Let's try that again. Are you ready?"

Melody took a deep breath. *Was she ready? Truly ready?*

"Yes," she said.

"Good."

Her mom spun her around to face the door.

"Then go get him."

CHAPTER 32

*M*elody exhaled, her breath visible in the cold night air.

She'd brought him outside to the back porch to tell him. He'd taken the news like a gentleman, as she'd known he would. There had been disappointment in his eyes, but also acceptance.

"You knew I had to try," he'd said.

"I'm glad you did," she'd replied.

"I think I get it. He seems like a good guy."

"I think so, too."

"I wish you every happiness."

"I wish the same for you."

Through the living room windows, she watched him rejoin the crowd gathered around the fireplace. Anna handed him a stick and a marshmallow. He gave her an appreciative grin, stuck the marshmallow on the stick, and held it over the fire.

Quietly, Melody slipped back inside.

One down, one to go.

She glanced around the living room but didn't see him. She went into the kitchen, but he wasn't there either.

So where *was* he?

Had he seen her head outside with his rival? Had he misinterpreted what that meant?

And if so, what would he do?

He'd be a gentleman about it. He'd want to avoid any awkwardness. He'd want to give her the space she needed.

She found him where she knew she'd find him: in the media room, standing at the work table. He had a saw in one hand and a piece of wood in the other, almost like he was trying to keep his feelings at bay by keeping himself busy.

He held her gaze as she walked toward him, his expression guarded.

"Hey," he said.

"Hey," she replied, the air thick with tension. When she reached the work table, he took a deep breath and set down the saw and piece of wood, clearly steeling himself for what she would say next.

"James," she began, then stopped as a wave of emotion snuck up on her. With a swallow, she pushed it back. "About Derek."

His shoulders tensed. "Yes?"

"You know why he came up here."

Silently, he nodded.

"He wanted to get back together."

"I know."

She took a deep breath, then said, "I told him no."

His eyes widened. "You did *what?*"

"And I told him why."

A surge of excitement — hope — flowed through him. "What was the reason why?"

"I told him I'd met someone."

His eyes widened. "Someone?"

"Someone special. Someone who feels so right. Someone who's promised me a proper first date."

Unable to restrain himself any longer, James rushed around the table and pulled her in close. His strong arms felt so wonderful around her, the heat of his body warming hers. "You better be talking about me."

She laughed and reached up and wrapped her arms around his neck. "Yes, I'm talking about you, James Newcastle."

He leaned in, his lips brushing hers, reveling in the moment.

When he kissed her, she leaped into the moment. Being with him felt so right and true. He was so strong, so passionate, so tender. There was a depth to this man — a solidity, a sense of purpose, a deeply caring nature, a passion for creativity matching hers. Her fears faded away as the universe pulled the curtain back and revealed a wide-open vista of joy and discovery.

He moved his lips to her ear. "You are so beautiful," he murmured. "So smart and wise and generous and gorgeous."

He pulled her even closer, his strength thrilling and reassuring all at once.

"I have a question," he said, his gaze full of wonder. "Artist to artist."

She felt a rush of pleasure at his words. "Ask away, fellow artist."

"What am I going to do when the rest of the world comes calling and whisks you away? When Broadway or Hollywood makes an offer you can't refuse?"

She smiled up at him, her voice soft. "We'll figure that out, one opportunity at a time. You did say you wanted to experience the big city."

He grinned. "You're right, I did say that."

"Besides, that question is a two-way street. What am I going to do when your furniture business takes off and suddenly you're dashing off to goodness-knows-where to work with clients?"

He chuckled, shaking his head. "Guess we'll figure that out, too."

"I can already see myself needing to pull you away from your buzz saw or jigsaw or whatever that thing there is called."

"That? That's just a regular old handsaw."

"Good thing I'm okay with sawdust."

He laughed and pulled her in tight. "Where should we go on our first date?"

"I happen to know a lovely cafe. They make delicious scones."

James laughed again, filling Melody with a warmth, a certainty, that had always eluded her.

Until now.

"Merry Christmas, James," she said, pulling him closer.

"Merry Christmas, Melody," he whispered back.

Then they kissed again, reveling in the assurance that when they leaped into their bright, shining future, they would be doing so — together.

THE END

Nick and the
Snowplow

A heartwarming holiday story about a handsome veterinarian and the shy, beautiful librarian he meets on Christmas Eve....

Nick and the Snowplow is a companion to *Christmas to the Rescue!*, the first novel in the Heartsprings Valley Winter Tale series. In *Christmas to the Rescue!*, a young librarian named Becca gets caught in a blizzard on Christmas Eve, finds shelter with a handsome veterinarian named Nick, and ends up experiencing the most surprising, adventure-filled night of her life.

Nick and the Snowplow, told from Nick's point of view, shows what happens after Nick brings Becca home at the end of their whirlwind evening.

This story is available FOR FREE when you sign up for Anne Chase's email newsletter.

Go to AnneChase.com to sign up and get your free story.

ALSO BY ANNE CHASE

AVAILABLE NOW OR COMING SOON

Heartsprings Valley Romances

Christmas to the Rescue!

A Very Cookie Christmas

Sweet Apple Christmas

I Dream of Christmas

Chock Full of Christmas

The Christmas Sleuth

Eagle Cove Mysteries

Murder So Deep

Murder So Cold

Murder So Pretty

Murder So Tender

Emily Livingston Mysteries

A Death in Barcelona

From Rome, With Murder

Paris Is for Killers

In London We Die

ABOUT THE AUTHOR

Greetings! I grew up in a small town (pop: 2,000) and now live in the bustling Bay Area. I write romances and mysteries, including:

The *Heartsprings Valley* romances: Celebrating love at Christmas in a small New England town.

The *Eagle Cove Mysteries:* An inquisitive cafe owner gets dragged into in murder and mayhem.

The *Emily Livingston Mysteries:* Intrigue and danger amidst the glamour and beauty of Europe.

My email newsletter is a great way to find out about upcoming books. Go to **AnneChase.com** to sign up.

Thank you for being a reader!